The Promise of Palmettos

To Edwina,
Thank you so much for reading my book. I really hope you enjoy the story.
Sheryse Noelle DuBose

Chapter 1

Flashbulbs popped as digital images of the crime scene were captured from every angle. The body of a young man who looked to be in his early thirties was lying spread-eagled and face-up on the carpet with a permanently surprised expression frozen on his handsome face. There was a single gunshot wound to the victim's chest. Blood had spilled from the wound and pooled into a huge puddle on the linoleum black and white checkered floor. If that weren't horrible enough, the tiny office was in shambles. Papers were strewn about, the furniture had been turned over, and what looked to be a brand-new computer had been sent crashing to the floor.

The police chief again took sight of the body. Saddened by the young life that was cut short, he shook his head in disbelief and thought, *What a waste.*

"You think someone tried to rob the place?" asked one of the senior officers looking around at the mess.

In all of his thirty years on the force, even during the twenty-five he'd spent on the mainland police force, he'd never seen anything like this. His job mainly involved writing speeding tickets and answering an occasional call from the General Store when one of those rowdy Larson kids walked a *Little Debbie's* out of the store without paying for it. But this? This looked like a scene from *Matlock*, which he watched sometimes on television.

"Don't know Clyde," answered the chief taking his handkerchief and wiping the beads of perspiration from his forehead. "It's a real mess but doesn't look like anything's been taken."

"'Cept for his wallet," said a second younger officer who had put away his camera and was now searching the body with gloved hands. "Can't seem to find any ID."

"Wallace, did you happen to read the door?" The police chief sighed warily. "That's where you'll find the victim's name."

"How do we know that this is him and this isn't some guy that just happened to be in the wrong place at the wrong time?"

Wallace wasn't very bright, in fact he was usually a complete meathead, but this time he had a point. Before he called this poor guy's family, he needed to be certain that he had the right person. Most of the native islanders knew one another. Right now, he could think of one islander who would be able to make an immediate positive ID.

A commotion outside caused the three officers to look towards the door that led to the front office. The chief suspected that it was the newly promoted detective, Jefferson Pierce.

"Tell me it's not true!" A tall handsome, brown-skinned man shouted as he rushed into the small office.

In his haste getting to the crime scene, Jefferson passed a couple from the cleaning crew without seeing them, so he missed their solemn nods confirming what he'd heard over the police scanner: The office of the Oak Grove Building Inspector had been broken into and its occupant murdered.

"Jefferson, do you know this poor soul?" asked the police chief eying the look of sorrow on the young detective's face, as his eyes fell on the body.

Jefferson nodded as the tears flowed free. Rubbing his clean-shaven head he replied, "That's Delmar LaCrosse. We grew up together in Creekside. We were supposed to meet tonight for drinks on the mainland, but I had to cancel because I had to catch up on some paperwork. What happened?"

"We was hopin' you could tell us," said Clyde who had little trust for this young imbecile who thought he could just become a detective after only a couple of years on the police force. "Ain't you the hotshot detective? Ain't that why they pay you the big bucks?"

"There's no sign of forced entry," said Jefferson looking around. "It looks like something is missing from this wall." Jefferson pointed at a wall at the far end of the office where only the outline of a 20 by 24 size space remained. "But I wouldn't call this a robbery though. The computer is still here although it's smashed on the floor."

He leaned over with great difficulty and examined the remains of his close friend.

"It looks like Delmar was shot at close range," Jefferson said observing the stippling around the wound. "He knew his attacker."

"How do you know that?" asked Officer Wallace.

"Look at this wound. Plus, Delmar would never let a stranger get this close to him."

Jefferson straightened up. "I'll go tell the family."

"Do you want me to do it?"

Jefferson looked at Chief Roger Dorfler. He was an older man in his fifties. His physique was short and squat. His hair was balding and what was left at the fringes was white making his already pale face look even paler.

Chief had been on the island about ten years but he was still considered a newcomer. Native Oak Grove Islanders had very little trust for newcomers. For this reason, Jefferson knew that he needed to be the one to make the dreaded late-night visit. Besides, Delmar was his friend. He couldn't save him from whatever evil got him, but he could at least be the one to tell his family.

"Thanks Chief, but I think it would be better coming from me."

Chapter 2

Lauren Malone peeked in on her two-year-old son, Justin, who was fast asleep in his bed. He looked like an angel now as if he hadn't spent the day running, climbing, and jumping all over the house. Justin was like that pink bunny on the commercial that kept on going. And Lauren, who was for the time being, a stay-at-home mom, had to go right along with him. By eight o'clock, which was Justin's bedtime, Lauren was usually beyond exhausted and today was no exception.

Lauren had spent the rest of the evening with her head on her husband, Kyle's shoulder watching reality television. It was their nightly tradition. Tonight was *America's Next Top Model* night and when the program was over, Lauren made one of her checks to see that the covers hadn't been kicked to the floor or that the toddler wasn't half hanging off the bed. Justin had remained properly under his covers so she just bent over to give him a kiss on his soft, brown, cheek. Under the moonlight, Lauren couldn't help but to study at him. He looked like Kyle now with his eyes closed. When he was awake, Justin was a splitting image of his mother, with his bright, brown eyes surrounded by long lashes and button nose. His mouth however, was Kyle's. Justin had his father's full lips and infectious smile. He had his father's build also, which was solid and strong.

There was so much to teach Justin about life, his heritage, and how especially to be a man who would one day have to provide for his own family. It was a huge job; one that Lauren and Kyle was determined to get right.

Satisfied that her baby boy was just fine, Lauren pulled Justin's door closed, walked back across the hall to the Master bedroom and straight into her closet to change out of her t-shirt and jeans, which seemed to be her uniform these days. As she folded her clothes she thought how much her life had changed over the last couple of years.

Lauren went to the bathroom to wash her face and caught a glimpse of herself in the mirror. She looked the same. She was a considerably attractive, brown-skinned woman. Kyle constantly told her that she was beautiful. Looking at herself, Lauren didn't think she lived up to 'beautiful' at the moment. Right now, she thought she could just pass for cute with her light brown eyes and full lips. Her thick brown hair was pulled into the usual ponytail. Her hair needed to be out of her face when running after Justin all day. She looked young for her age, a gene that she was fortunate to receive from both sides of her family, but she felt a lot older. Motherhood did that sometimes. Lauren took one last look before leaving the bathroom. Whew, she needed to make a hair appointment to get her split ends under control immediately! She walked back into the bedroom to find that Kyle had come upstairs from the living room.

"Is Justin asleep?" he asked not looking up from the stack of bills he was making his way through at the desk.

"Out like a light," said Lauren slipping under covers. She let out a sigh as her body was finally allowed to relax.

"Good," said Kyle as he logged an entry into the spreadsheet that was displayed on the computer. "Did you find anything today?"

This had been his routine question for the past six-months, ever since the couple moved to Macon.

"There is nothing. I simply cannot find any planning jobs in this area," Lauren answered with frustration.

Lauren and Kyle both had a degree in urban and regional planning but Kyle left the profession and seized what the couple thought to be a once-in-a-lifetime opportunity. He partnered with an old friend from school to start a development company that specialized in redeveloping homes in urban neighborhoods.

The Malones moved from Tennessee with the hope that Lauren, with her vast experience in planning, would land a position quickly. It had been a half a year with only two interviews, neither of which panned out to anything. Kyle, on numerous occasions, offered Lauren a job with his firm but she was determined to stay in the planning field and work for a local government. Kyle respected her decision and remained supportive as she perused the planning sites and the government web pages, and sent off countless resumes to which she'd received no responses.

"What about the counties south of Atlanta?" Kyle asked as he had been asking every day.

"There's nothing Kyle."

"Don't give up hope, Lor," said Kyle reaching for the checkbook. "Business is doing well, so it's not like you need to work."

"I *do* need to work, Kyle. I love being a mother, but a housewife and a mother is not all that I am. You married a woman with ambition and goals. Justin is two. He doesn't need a full-time mommy anymore."

"I know what you're saying, Sweetie but the Lord works everything out in his own time. Maybe He wants you to be just a mother for now. I mean look at our son. I've never seen a happier, well-adjusted boy."

"I appreciate that Kyle," said Lauren as the telephone rang. "I just need to have more patience."

Lauren reached across the bed for the telephone on her husband's end table.

"Hello?" said Lauren absently into the receiver. "Oh hey, Dad."

Kyle looked at the clock. It was a quarter to eleven. Lauren's parents never called this late. As if to confirm Kyle's concerns, Lauren began screaming and crying until she couldn't speak anymore.

Kyle was at her side in an instant. "Lauren what is it?!"

But Lauren was too hysterical to answer, so Kyle grabbed the phone from her.

"Dad?" Kyle spoke into the receiver.

"Hello Kyle," John LaCrosse sounded very sad on the other end.

"What's going on?"

"We got some bad news. Delmar was found shot dead in his office."

"No! Oh no!" Kyle cried as he held on tightly to his wife, who was sobbing in his chest.

"Kyle, I'm depending on you to take care of Lauren. You know how close she and Delmar were."

"I know that as well as anyone," Kyle said as tears streamed down his own face. "That's why we'll be headed for Oak Grove first thing tomorrow morning.

Chapter 3

Lauren hardly said two words as she, Kyle, and little Justin packed up the car to make the five-hour trip to Oak Grove, a Sea Island off the coast of South Carolina. What was so special about the Sea Islands is that its isolation was conducive to preserving West African language, cultivation methods, and customs that had been otherwise lost in other American settlements. Of course Lauren had taken all of this for granted while growing up. If it were not for occasional visits to her mother's people down on the southern islands, Lauren would have had very limited knowledge of life off of Oak Grove. When she got to undergraduate school, she'd felt out of place among her fellow students, most of whom had hailed from large cities. It was Lauren's history professor who had detected a slight trace of a Sea Island accent in her speech. Having given a doctoral dissertation on the preservation of Gullah culture on the Sea Islands, Dr. Susana Marx was all too happy to give her young student an impromptu history lesson of her culture, giving Lauren a sense of pride in her heritage.

Going to Oak Grove Island was like traveling back in time before paved roads, congestion, and mass development. Just thinking about the island stirred up images of crashing waves and tall palmetto trees with its long, green, leaves blowing in the breeze. Lauren could remember the feel of the rough bark of the also prominent oak trees, from when she, Delmar, and Netta spent the summer days climbing trees, their hands and faces sticky from the icy pop they bought from the General Store.

Oak Grove Island had not yet been touched by development but it was coming, just as it had come to all of the other Sea Islands along the coast. After they built the drawbridge that connected Oak Grove with the modern world, it was only a matter of time. When the developers did arrive, they needed to be ready, Delmar would always tell her. For that reason, the two first cousins entered planning school. Lauren went to the University of New Orleans and Delmar to Alabama A and M.

Ironically, it was Delmar who had introduced Lauren to Kyle, his close friend and roommate. She'd come up to Huntsville for the Homecoming their first year in school and the three of them went to the game together.

"Wow, there's nothing like Homecoming at a Historically Black College!" Lauren had commented as she did a little dance in place while the band got their jam on. "There's more partying in the stands than actual game watching!"

"What, you guys don't get down like that at UNO?" Kyle had asked her. He was one of the few people who were actually interested in the game.

"Are you kidding?" Lauren looked at Kyle with an incredulous look "We don't even have a football team!"

"I told you to come to A and M with me," Delmar had laughed at her. "That way you won't be missing out."

"Who says I'm missing out?" Lauren swatted her cousin on his arm. "First of all, I like New Orleans. Second, I had plenty of good homecoming games in undergrad, and third, I will be going to Mardi Gras. I heard that is off the hook!"

"Where did you go to undergrad?" Kyle had asked before Delmar could argue back.

Lauren had smiled at Kyle warmly, taking in his friendly eyes and teasing grin. "I went to Hampton."

Kyle fixed his mouth in an expression that reflected he was impressed. "Oh Hampton. Good school."

"Yes it is."

"So you are no stranger to Homecoming partying."

"Uh-uh." Lauren turned to Kyle giving him a flirtatious look then asked, "So you know of any after parties we can get into?"

Kyle had given her a flirty look of his own. "I can think of a few places."

Lauren, feeling quite warm under Kyle's gaze, slipped out of her light blue windbreaker.

"Whatchu got a UNO shirt on for?" Delmar pointed to his cousin's dark blue and white t-shirt.

Lauren put her hand on her hip, "Well maybe if you bought me an A and M shirt like I've been asking for since school started, I coulda worn that! Besides, what difference does it make, I'm still routing for you guys."

But Delmar shook his head in mock disappointment. "Where's the loyalty?"

Lauren just rolled her eyes.

Delmar noticed the obvious chemistry between Lauren and Kyle and told the two that that he "forgot" a date he'd made earlier then left Kyle and Lauren together. They never did make it to the parties. Instead they had dinner and spent all evening talking as if they'd known each other their entire lives. By the time the weekend was over, Kyle had bought Lauren her A and M t-shirt. Five years later, Delmar was the best man at their wedding.

"Did I tell you about the time we snuck out to go crabbing out behind Aunt Eleanor's house?" Lauren suddenly spoke, breaking through Kyle's memories.

"I don't think I heard that one," said Kyle, happy that his wife had some good memories to share.

"Well we were all staying the night at Grandmama's. You know she has that screened porch that looks out onto the ocean. I can still remember how the smell of the sea air and the sound of the waves crashing could put a body to sleep instantly."

"I can imagine," Kyle smiled at her.

"Well Netta wasn't trying to sleep that night. She kept saying that the creek had 12-foot crabs in it."

"12-*foot* crabs?" Kyle exclaimed laughing. "How is that possible?"

"Of course Delmar and I thought she was lying but she insisted she was telling the truth. So we did what all ten-year-olds did: We told her to prove it."

"How did you do that?" asked Kyle.

"We snuck out, got the crabbing nets out of the shed – my granddaddy used to weave those himself – and rode our bikes out to the creek, which was a good two or three miles. When we got to the creek we realized we didn't have any bait. Delmar sees the little crab holes in the marsh so he comes up with the idea to dig them up for bait. We had to wade through the marsh anyway to get to the creek. So we're looking for bait and Delmar sticks his foot in some of that extra squishy mud and gets his foot stuck. It's sucking him down and the more he tries to pull himself out, the more stuck he gets. Netta and I tug on his leg to get it out but it was really sucking him down. We were so scared that it was quicksand because that mud got a hold of him and didn't want to let go. Finally, when we did manage to get his leg out, the mud had sucked his sneaker right off of his foot. So we started digging and we couldn't find it because the more we dug, the more the mud closed over it. We would have never known his foot had even been there had we not seen it for ourselves. That sneaker was just gone and Delmar knew he was in trouble because they were brand new.

Now of course we should have gone back when Delmar lost his sneaker but Netta insisted that we continue on."

"Then what happened?" asked Kyle just as they reached the sign that says, *South Carolina Welcomes You.* "Did you catch your 12-foot crab?"

"We might have, but we'll never know."

"Why not?"

"We'd fallen asleep on the banks of the creek and were awakened by our parents and grandparents yelling at us. They'd snatched us away before we could check the traps."

Kyle laughed again. "How much trouble did you get into?"

"Lots! We couldn't sit down for a good week after they all got finished with us," Lauren laughed. It was the first time she'd laughed since receiving the news about Delmar.

"I bet you three didn't have any more late night adventures after that."

"Not so much," Lauren said soberly and the smile melted from her face. Her eyes looked sad again. "Not too long after that, Netta's parents got into some trouble and she had to go live with her grandparents, Micah and Eleanor. Remember that Netta is our third cousin. Great Uncle Micah adored Netta and her sisters, but Aunt Eleanor made their lives a living hell. It was even worse after Great Uncle Micah died."

"When did he die?"

"When we were about 13, I guess," Lauren said. "From that point on, Netta didn't hang out with us as much. We were together at school, but we didn't have any more slumber parties. We weren't as close anymore either."

"That's a shame," said Kyle as he pulled off the exit to stop for gas.

"Yeah," Lauren sighed. "It really is."

Chapter 4

After Lauren had gotten the news about Delmar, sleep for her had been out of the question. The pain was so great she could barely stand it. Lauren had spent much of the night lying awake staring out of her bedroom window at the full moon, her mind busy with thoughts of Delmar and who could have done this to him. By the time the orange, yellow, and pink lights of morning filtered in through the blinds, she was crying again, muffling her sobs with a pillow. She didn't want to wake Kyle, who'd manage to finally drift off himself around 2:30 in the morning.

Now in the car, a couple of hours away from Oak Grove, Lauren succumbed to a restless sleep. In her dreams, Delmar was still alive and they were children again, laughing and running though the high, white sand dunes towards the water. She, Delmar, and Netta were splashing salt water at each other and jumping over the frothy-looking waves...

Lauren woke with a start. The beach was gone and she was in the car. Remembering that Delmar was dead crashed down on Lauren like a ton of bricks. She longed to go back to her dreams where Delmar was still alive and laughing. But it would be just a dream. In reality, her cousin was gone and Lauren longed to find the reason.

Looking out of her window, Lauren noticed that they were about 30 miles from Oak Grove. One clue that they were reaching the coastal area was the abundance of trees with leaves so plush that they blocked out the sun as they traveled along the two-lane road. Every once in a while, there would be a break in the foliage and the rays of sunlight would filter through. Had the Malones traveled at night, the only light on that dark road would have been from their headlights. And like the sun in the daytime, if the moon was full, it would reflect off of the waters in the marshes that would suddenly appear between the trees, providing temporary light before hiding in the darkness once more.

During the last few miles to Oak Grove Island, Lauren would always be filled with a sense of anticipation and excitement, knowing that she would be seeing her family within the hour. The road always seemed longer, the trees even more dense, and there was always that car in front of theirs that seemed go more slowly than the law allowed. Lauren wasn't feeling that excitement now. Now, she had a sense that all the special things that made this Sea Island home died the right along with Delmar. All too soon, the Malones pulled up right in front of the wooden, two-story, 1970s style home. Even the strong loving embrace from each of her parents did very little to comfort Lauren's broken heart.

Chapter 5

Delmar's grave was located in Oak Creek Cemetery. The cemetery was located next to Oak Creek, which was one of the many creeks that wove its way through the fifteen-mile island. It was the tradition of the Gullah natives to bury their dead near the water, for it was believed that water was the gateway into Heaven.

To non-island natives, this final resting place was just a collection of trees and shrub easily overlooked by passersby. Upon closer observation, headstones dating back to as early as the 19th century could be found among the tall and majestic oaks that were older than the cemetery itself.

Lauren took comfort that Delmar would be in good company. Granddad Lazarus and Uncle Micah, whose graves were nearby, would watch after him. As the family gathered around the open grave, heart-broken sobs punctuated the normally quiet grounds. The words of Pastor Lockhart provided some comfort as the family tried to find understanding in the brutal slaying of their loved one.

Aunt Dinah and Uncle Thomas, Delmar's parents, grasped tightly to each other as if not to let the other slip away. His two sisters, walking hand in hand, gently placed white roses on their brother's coffin and the rest of the family followed suit. Lauren kissed the petal of her white rose before gently laying it down on top of the others. Then she reached for Kyle and the two of them crying softly, left the gravesite.

As the family turned to leave, a piercing scream felt as though it ripped through Lauren's very soul. She and Kyle, as well as the rest of the family, turned towards Delmar's mother, Dinah. Though her face was streaked with silent tears, the scream had not come from her. She too looked on as Lauren's father, John and his brothers were instantly by their mother's side. Poor Grandma Henrietta had thrown herself across Delmar's casket, sobbing hysterically.

"Lord Jesus, why?!" she screamed.

John gently tried to pull his mother away from Delmar, but she wrenched herself away.

"God forgive me," she whimpered before going limp in John's arms. She allowed him to lead her away from the gravesite of her oldest grandson to one of the waiting cars that would take her home for the repast.

God forgive her? Lauren thought. *Why would Grandma ask for God to forgive her?*

Chapter 6

"That was a very lovely service," said Aunt Tessie, a tall and rather shapely woman. The silk lavender dress she wore complimented her butter pecan brown skin. Matching low-heeled shoes completed her outfit. Her light brown hair (the grays were hidden with reddish brown highlights) was twisted expertly into a French roll. As she never had to worry about putting on weight, even in her middle age, she dished up a heaping amount of macaroni and cheese onto her plate.

They were all at Grandma Henrietta's house. After her outburst in the cemetery, Grandma had gone straight to her room to rest, so her daughters served as the hostesses instead.

"Yes it was," responded Aunt Philomena. The oldest sister, she was a tall, full-figured, brown-skinned woman dressed to the nines as usual. Today, she wore a simple black, silk, wrap-around dress that accentuated her small waste. A large wide-brim black hat sat neatly and carefully on top of her thick hair. Balancing expertly on black high-heeled pumps, she walked over to the end of the table and grabbed a paper plate. She was headed for the platter of catfish freshly caught and fried up that morning. "Pastor Lockhart had some wonderful things to say about Delmar."

"Yes he did," said Aunt Tessie, then she asked, "Did the police tell Thomas and Dinah anything else about the case?"

Tessie spied the collard greens and managed to grab the serving spoon before Cousin Trina ("Dang Aunt Tessie! You almost took out an eye!") who then shifted her direction towards the homemade cornbread.

Lauren and Kyle knew from experience to stand clear of these women anytime there was a buffet. They loved food and would mow over anyone to fill their plate first. The couple stood aside with their paper plates and waited for the aunts to finish helping themselves. They all greeted Great Aunt Eleanor as she passed by, making her way to the back rooms towards Grandma Henrietta's room.

"They still investigatin'," Aunt Philomena responded to Aunt Tessie's question. "That what Theresa told me this morning."

Theresa was one of Delmar's younger sisters.

"Well how long is it gonna take them to find out who did this to Delmar! Don't them no-count police know that the family wants answers?" Aunt Tessie asked riled up. Her plate was so full that Lauren didn't know where she was going to even add the lima beans she'd just scooped out of the steaming pot. Tessie solved the problem by plopping them on top of her cornbread. It was all going to the same place anyway.

"Tessie, you need to be quiet," said Aunt Philomena, lowering her voice and looking around. "Dinah's right in the next room. This is already hard on her and we don't want to her more upset than she already is."

"I don't see how that's possible, Philomena. She done already lost her only son. Ain't no more upset she can get 'bout that."

Lauren had enough of this conversation, so she handed her still empty plate to Kyle and stormed into the kitchen almost whacking Netta in the face with the swinging door.

"Hey Netta!" Lauren reached up to give her cousin a big hug.

"It's good to see you, Lor," said Netta somberly, returning the hug.

"Sorry about the door," Lauren apologized after they let go.

"No problem."

Lauren took in her cousin's appearance. Her makeup, as usual, was flawless, accentuating her high cheekbones and full lips. The LaCrosse lips were the one trait she and Lauren shared. Netta had always been tall. In fact Lauren, who was barely 5 foot 3, had always been jealous of her height. What Netta had in height however, she lacked in hair. Lauren had always been the blessed one in that department. It was both long and thick, styled in either a ponytail or on special occasions, curls. Today, however Netta had Lauren's simple, shoulder-length, bob hairstyle beat also. The sharp new hair weave was cut into long layers and fell past her shoulders. The red highlights gleamed under the glow of the kitchen light.

Kyle pushed the kitchen door open and handed Lauren a plate full of food and a drink.

"Figured to dish you up a plate while the coast is clear."

Lauren took the plate from him. "Thanks, I couldn't listen to that anymore. I just had to get out of there."

Kyle noticed Netta leaning against the sink. "Hey Netta." He gave her a warm hug.

"Kyle, it's good to see you."

Kyle let go of Netta and said, "I'll leave the two of you to catch up." He headed back out into the dining room to dish up his own plate.

"How you doin', girl?" Netta asked Lauren when they were alone again.

Lauren sighed "Not well. I can't believe he's gone."

"Me neither. I half expect him to walk in through the door with that lopsided grin of his and ask what the hell we're doing and why come we didn't invite him to dinner."

Though Lauren gave a small chuckle, she felt the tears gather behind her eyes. She didn't want to start crying again, she'd done too much of that already, so she changed the subject.

"What are you up to these days?"

"Don't you know? I started my own real estate company. Got my license and everything. I thought Del would have told you."

"He didn't tell me!" Lauren exclaimed. "I'm so proud of you. I knew you could be successful if you just had focus!"

"Well damn, Lauren. Just because I've been in trouble doesn't mean I'm a hopeless case." Netta had suddenly turned sullen.

"Oh come on, Netta," Lauren protested. "You know I didn't mean it that way. Del and I always knew you were smarter than Aunt Eleanor gave you credit."

"Whatever. Like you even know about it. You and Delmar were raised by parents who loved you and cared for you. They helped you with your homework and thought about your futures. My parents only thought about planning the next liquor store heist. Maybe if my parents were more like yours, they wouldn't have gotten locked up and I would have had to be raised by mean ol' grandmother!"

Lauren was instantly sorry that she got Netta started. She and Delmar had to listen to the "woe is me" tirade ever since they were teenagers. There was only one way to stop her once she got going.

"Netta, I'm sorry," said Lauren, hoping that her apology would do the trick. Fortunately for her nerves, the trick worked.

"Me too," Netta replied calming down. "I'm just on edge."

"I understand," Lauren responded although she knew if they were at a wedding reception rather than a wake, it would be the same thing all over again.

"You find a job in Macon?" Netta asked.

"No. Not yet. There's really not a huge market for urban planners in Middle Georgia."

"I don't know how you and Delmar could do that planning stuff. It don't seem like you can do a whole lot with it."

"Sure you can," said Lauren, trying to keep her temper.

She knew that Netta was jealous because while she had been in and out of trouble, Lauren and Delmar were busy getting their degrees. It gave Netta one more reason to feel left out. It had not been the cousins' intention to leave Netta out of their plans to study planning, but when they approached her about getting a graduate degree (In Netta's case, first getting an undergraduate degree) in order to fulfill "The Promise," she wasn't even trying to hear that.

"Look, you can go and get a million degrees to achieve some pie-in-the-sky dream if you want to," she had said with a fierce attitude. "But my school days are done. Leave me out of it. I've got a husband to tend to and a child to raise."

And Lauren and Delmar did exactly that. They'd left her out of it because as Lauren would find herself constantly saying in all their years together, "She's not ready."

"Urban planners do all sorts of things," Lauren continued as she poured herself some homemade lemonade. "We develop and organize neighborhoods, we help citizens decide where to put homes and businesses, we place roads and highways. The list is endless."

"You don't decide all that. A bunch of old fogies make that decision."

Lauren couldn't really argue with that. If she had a nickel for every time the planning commission went against her recommendations, she could take yearly vacations in the South of France for the rest of her life.

"No, I don't always get things to go the way I think it's supposed to, but I enjoy being a planner and so did Delmar."

"How long you gonna be on the island?" Netta changed the subject again.

"A couple of days," Lauren responded, also glad that Netta didn't want to continue this conversation. She had a feeling that it wouldn't have ended well.

"Good. Then let's have lunch."

"Sure. Call me with the when and where."

Lauren made her way into the living room where about twenty relatives were squeezed on sofas, chairs, and along the walls. Kyle pointed to the empty spot on the sofa he'd vacated when he saw her coming and Lauren found herself squeezed in between her mother and her younger sister, Cara.

"Have those rascals been by your house yet?" asked Uncle Izzie, Aunt Philomena's husband. He was clearly agitated because he kept scratching his bushy beard, the only hair on his round face.

Uncle Izzie was a big man testing out the weight of one of Grandma Henrietta's old armchairs. He had to sit at the edge of it in order to spread his legs to a comfortable width. Lauren could see he'd already lost the battle with his black pants as he'd already torn a hole in the crotch. Cara also noticed and kept jabbing her older sister in the ribs with her elbow. Lauren refused to look back at her for fear she would laugh out loud and embarrass all of them.

"What rascals, Iz?" asked a man in an extremely loud canary yellow suit, who Lauren did not know, but suspected was family. She guessed the plump woman with the red hat sitting next to him was his wife.

"This guy came by our door last Friday and handed us a business card talking about he can offer us a fair price for our land." The conversation was starting to get interesting and Lauren was successfully able to focus on it and not on Uncle Izzie's red and white polka dot draughs that were becoming more and more visible.

"Oh really now?"

"Yes sirree. I told him that my property wasn't for sale. Hell, I sell to him, where am I gonna live?

"Ya know?" A couple of responses, punctuated by chuckles came from around the room.

"How much he offer? Shoot you can buy a new place to live, it be enough," the man responded.

"Are you crazy?!" Uncle Izzie exclaimed as he sat straight up. The chair groaned in protest beneath his weight. "Do you know what them white people are doing on them islands to the south? They buy up all the property from black folks and make it so that we can't afford to get back on the island and live in the luxury that they built. They don't want people who look like us on the islands now unless you cookin' their meals and servin' their food.

Hell, even now they gettin' them Spanish people for them jobs."

"So you count yo' money and move somewhere else, ain't that right, Eleanor?"

Aunt Eleanor had just come out of Henrietta's room. "Leave me out of this, I gotta 'tend to my watermelon, now," she said.

"Can't you leave that for another day?" asked the man. "That watermelon ain't goin' nowhere," he said.

"Well it ain't gonna tend itself!" Aunt Eleanor came back at him as she walked out the front door. It slammed shut behind her.

"Yeah, you over here whining about the white folks. We got something they want and they gonna pay if they want to have it," said the man laughing. "Play your cards right and you can be as rich as them."

"I know that's right," agreed the woman with the red hat sitting next to him. When she opened her mouth to laugh, Lauren noticed that her front tooth had a gold star.

"Now that's some ig'nant thinkin', School Boy," Uncle Izzie came back. "You sell off your property, what you gonna have to leave to your kids?"

"Man, my kids are scattered to the four winds. They ain't comin' back here 'cause they say there ain't nothin' for them to come back to."

"And there really ain't gonna be nothing for them to come back to if we sell off everything we own!"

"Whatever, man. Some guy come to my door offerin' me a million dollars for my five acres, I'm gonna take it that's for damn sure. You do what you wanna!"

"You just do that," John spoke up, his strong voice carried clearly across the room. "But I don't want to see your ugly mug on CNN talking about how the white man stole your land. Furthermore, if you accept only a million dollars for those five acres that is located only a mile away from the beach, you might as well say that they have stolen it."

"But isn't that what they're doing?" Cousin Trina spoke up. She'd finished her two helpings of food and now she joined the large group in the living room, leaning against the wall under the large portrait of Lazarus and Henrietta. "Ain't they jacking up the prices of the land so high that no one can afford to stay on these islands even if you don't sell?"

"I don't deny that," John responded. "I'm just saying that it is time that we take some responsibility for what is going on with these islands. We need to work harder to hold onto what is rightfully ours. Let me ask you all something: Why is it that every other nationality that comes to this country and establishes their Chinatowns, Little Italys, Little Cubas, Korea Towns, and whatever else in every city and are able to maintain their language and their culture? It's because they understand the importance of keeping their heritage alive and having something to give to the next generation. Nothing will make them budge from these areas. Then there is us. Some bigwig comes along and offers us money, and we give away everything with both hands. Now what does that tell you?"

Everyone shook their heads in agreement. As usual, John made perfect sense. That is he made sense to everyone but the one called 'School Boy'. "That tells me them white folks ain't offerin' them Chinese, Italians, Cubans, and Koreans enough money!"

"See? That's why we ain't gonna have nothin' 'cause *some fools*," Uncle Izzie looked pointedly at School Boy, "think someone with a checkbook is gonna give 'em somethin' better 'n they already got!"

There was no changing School Boy's mind. He made it perfectly clear that he was selling his land at the first opportunity.

All John could do was shake his head then change the subject to who had a chance in the NBA playoffs.

Chapter 7

"Daddy, who was that guy at Grandma's house, yesterday?" Lauren asked the next morning as she jammed her foot into her blue and white sneaker.

"What guy?" asked John, who was fiddling around with the coffeemaker.

Her father was a tall and sinewy man. In spite of the flecks of grey in his hair, John LaCrosse still looked like a young man. In fact, the grey only made him looked more distinguished. If Lauren had to describe her father in one word it would be "wise". It was evident in the way he talked to people, but it could be seen in his eyes as well. John looked at people as if he could see right through them. It was for that reason Lauren had a difficult time telling her father an untruth. The other reason is that when she was a girl, he would have skinned her alive for lying.

Nevertheless, Lauren thought the sun rose and set on her father. Until Kyle came along, no other man could come close to him. Except for Delmar.

"The one who wanted to sell his land for a million dollars." Lauren jammed her other foot in then went to the refrigerator for some orange juice.

"Oh that guy!" John laughed. "That was School Boy."

"Skull Boy?" Lauren wrinkled her nose with distaste. She poured her juice into a small glass and took a sip.

"No *School* Boy. His real name is Erwin Mays, but people have been calling him 'School Boy' for as long as I can remember. He's like a distant cousin."

"Why on earth would he be named School Boy? Is he smart or something? I don't think he is by the way he sounded last night."

"Smart? Hardly. In fact he's the dumbest cat I'd ever laid my eyes on. The boy was in still in the 11th grade when I got there."

Lauren laughed as she put a blueberry muffin in the microwave and set the timer for a couple of seconds.

"What are you doing up so early?" asked John as he fixed two cups of coffee.

One was for him and the other was for his wife, Marne, who was still upstairs. Marne refused to put one toe out of bed until she had at least one cup of coffee.

Lauren watched the muffin revolve on the turn table a couple of seconds before deciding that it was ready. She opened the microwave door to retrieve it before answering her father.

"Kyle and I are going to drive around the island for a little while. Do you guys mind looking after Justin?"

"Mind? Looking after our only grandson? Of course we don't mind!"

"Thanks Dad."

Lauren and Kyle took off down the dirt road fifteen minutes later. The couple took in the sights as they passed by landmarks familiar to Lauren. They drove through Creekside, Lauren and Delmar's side of the island. There was the old General Store on the right, where she, Delmar, and Netta had gotten more than their share of icy pops to cool them off during the hot summer days. It was a small, wooden building that barely had enough room for three customers. Mr. Elway Curtis, who Lauren could see through the window standing in front of the cash register, seemed to be old even when the kids were young. Lauren was relieved to see him standing there like he had been for years. His presence was familiar and familiarity was something that Lauren needed to help ease the empty feeling. It helped some, but not a whole lot. As usual, the dirt parking lot in front of the store was full.

Maylene's Crab shack was coming up also on the right side. Overlooking Blue Creek, Maylene pulled her crabs out of the water from the back porch and boiled them up right there. She served them up with hush puppies, sweet potato chips, and a side of good music. On Friday and Saturday nights, her restaurant was full of folks who just wanted a change of pace after working all week.

Kyle made a right and the winding road took them towards the beach. This section of the island was called

"Beachfront" for obvious reasons. Lauren pressed the button to roll down the window and the sea air instantly filled their noses.

"We should stop by Grandma's house since we're out here," said Lauren. "I want to see how she's doing."

"I think that we should," Kyle agreed. "I think yesterday was pretty rough on her especially."

Kyle parked the car in Henrietta's grassy yard and the two of them got out. Tree cover was less abundant on this side of the island and the bright rays from the sun beamed down on them immediately. Shielding her eyes, Lauren took sight of the sand dunes a few yards away. Though she could not see it from where she was standing, the mighty Atlantic made its presence known as the sound of the waves could be heard slamming against the shore. Dad and Uncle Izzie were right, Lauren decided. There are some things that money couldn't buy.

"We should take Justin to the beach before we leave," she said.

"He'd like that," Kyle answered. "Come on, let's see if Grandma's home."

The two of them made their way around the back of the small white house of sea shells mixed in mortar, towards the screen porch - the same screen porch where she, Delmar, and Netta had spent so many nights. They let themselves onto the porch and Lauren knocked on the heavy, wooden door. All was quiet except for the sounds of the waves and seagulls in the short distance. Lauren knocked again.

"Grandma!" Lauren called out in case she couldn't hear the knocks.

The Promise of Palmettos

"Maybe she's not home," Kyle offered.

"Maybe not," Lauren said hesitantly. "I hope she's okay."

"Sure she is. You know how your grandmother can't sit still for too long. One of the sisters could have taken her to the market." Kyle reasoned, speaking of Henrietta's daughters who sometimes helped her run errands.

"You're right," said Lauren decidedly. Kyle took her by the hand and the two of them walked back to the car.

The couple's back was turned so they did not see the rustling of the curtains in one of the windows.

"Let's take the Spanish Oak Road back," said Lauren who was enjoying the drive.

"You're the boss," Kyle responded cheerfully and made the left turn at the stop sign.

The Spanish Oak Road, named most likely for the abundance of oak trees draped with long strands of Spanish moss, was unpaved as many of the roads were on Oak Grove Island. It led to the center of the island called Creekside, where farming land was still plentiful. As a girl, Lauren liked to look out at the neat rows and rows of tomato, cucumber, corn, and other fruits and vegetables, sprouting from the earth that stretched as far as the eye could see. The farmers would take their crops to the mainland to sell at the market place and that was one of the ways many of the islanders earned their living. Fishing had been the other staple. Some families like the LaCrosses made their living also selling homemade quilts, woven fishing nets, and baskets.

Lauren's parents, John and Marne, who taught high school and grade school, respectively, were one of the few professional people who remained on Oak Grove. As the older islanders were replaced by the younger, farming and fishing became less prevalent. Some even sought new opportunities elsewhere. Many as children had spent their lives in the field. They had no desire to do it as adults. So many farmlands were eventually replaced by trees and underbrush that grew thicker with the passing seasons.

Fishing was now for sport and leisure rather than a way to earn a living. Many times Lauren and her family would wade out from Grandma's property into waste-high water to catch fish out of the Atlantic Ocean. John would always tease the family about catching their dinner. It was desperate times when ten people were eating (Delmar's family along with Netta would usually join them on the fishing trips) and there were only four fish swimming in the bucket. Crabbing was best from LaCrosse Creek that served as the dividing line between Grandma Henrietta's and Aunt Eleanor's property, and fed into the Sweet Brush River. No, they wouldn't catch a 12-foot crab as Netta had boasted a long time ago, but the ones they did catch were particularly large and succulent.

The first time Kyle had tasted a crab that was caught from LaCrosse Creek, he thought he'd died and gone to Heaven. It was simply the best crab he'd ever tasted. In fact, he refused to leave Oak Grove Island each visit without a freshly caught seafood meal.

"Kyle stop!" Lauren's outburst quickly brought Kyle out of his reverie.

Kyle quickly slammed on the brakes causing clouds of dust to rise up through the open windows, "What?! What's wrong?!"

"Look!"

Lauren pointed out of the window. Kyle followed her finger to the sold sign that was firmly planted into the ground. "That's the Robinson property. Or it *was* the Robinson property."

"Yeah, I see it," Kyle responded relieved that the cause for Lauren's outburst wasn't more serious.

"When Delmar visited us a couple of weeks ago, he told me this was happening, but to see it with my own eyes...Nevermind. Just keep driving."

Kyle put the car in gear and they drove further down the road. They had not gone a mile when Lauren spotted another "sold" sign on the left.

"That's the Harrison property. The Smith family too?!" Lauren exclaimed as Kyle swerved to avoid hitting a white SUV.

Lauren spied three more sold properties on the Spanish Oak Road. "All that land," she groaned.

"I know it's sad, Baby," said Kyle patiently. "But you're going to see more of this happening as development makes its way into this area."

"And what is the Wessler-Forrest Corporation?"

"Who?"

"See on that sign that was by the road? I saw several signs on the sold properties with that name. Do you think that's who's buying up all of the properties?"

"That would be my guess," Kyle said as he turned the car towards home. "Uncle Izzie did say it was some big corporation that was interested in his land. Based on these large tracts that they've bought, I bet they're planning for some large scale development."

"That would be my guess too," Lauren agreed. "And if Uncle Izzie is right about Oak Grove looking like those southern islands, there won't be any more black folks here either."

Chapter 8

When Delmar came to visit us in Macon a few weeks ago on his way to Atlanta, didn't he tell you what was happening with the properties?" Kyle asked on the way back to Lauren's parents' house.

"Yes, he told me that people were selling off their land," Lauren answered distracted. She was still extremely bothered by the large acres of land that had been sold. The island was changing and she had a feeling that it was not for the better.

"How did he sound?" asked Kyle with a suspicious tone to his voice.

"What do you mean how did he sound?" asked Lauren impatient with her husband's question.

"I mean how did he sound? Was he worried? Sad? Mad? Did he just bring up the subject out of the blue?"

"Okay, if you really must know, we were talking about old times and he changed the subject and said something like, 'People have been approached about selling their properties and a few have actually gone through with it.'"

"And what did you say?" asked Kyle.

"Well I told him that it was horrible and asked him why they were selling."

"What did he say?"

"Come to think of it," Lauren remembered. "He got this weird look on his face like he was dying to tell me something but he said instead, 'Who knows.' Then Justin woke up from his nap and I had to go to him so I never got to question him further about it."

"Hmm...." Kyle said thinking.

Lauren immediately jumped on his thought train. "Do you think that Delmar stumbled onto something?" Lauren asked in alarm. "Do you think that's why he was murdered?"

"Another question you should ask yourself is how come Delmar came all the way down to Macon to see you on his way to Atlanta? That's 70 miles out of the way. I think he came to see you for a reason."

Lauren suddenly made up her mind.

"Head downtown," she told Kyle.

What Lauren had referred to as "downtown" was located on the island's southern end. The white islanders, what few there were, had only moved to Oak Grove within the last decade, occupying smaller beach front tracts. To establish island services, they'd paved their roads, laid down sewer lines, and created a downtown area, which consisted of one lone main street. Main Street was comprised of five weathered clapboard buildings that held the police station, town hall, courthouse, the magistrate's office, and the office of the building inspector – Delmar's office.

The couple hopped out of the car and went into the police station.

"Yes, may I help you?" asked a man with a crew cut, who Lauren took for the desk sergeant. He barely looked up from hunting and pecking out words on a computer keyboard that looked to be several decades old.

"We're here to see Jefferson Pierce," Lauren spoke up.

"May I ask what it's regarding?" He inquired still hunting and pecking.

"It's about the Delmar LaCrosse case."

"That is an on-going investigation. Were you called in by Detective Pierce to give a statement?"

Lauren and Kyle exchanged irritated glances. What was up with the twenty questions? Meanwhile, officer kept peck-peck-pecking away on his computer.

Kyle had had enough. "Look Officer…"

"Moody," he filled in, finally looking up from his keyboard at the couple.

"Officer Moody, we just want to see Detective Pierce. Is he in?"

"Lauren! Kyle!"

Lauren and Kyle looked towards the back of the office. Jefferson was waving them over.

"It's okay Clyde," he said to Officer Moody. "They're friends of mine and Lauren was Delmar's cousin."

Clyde just scowled at him.

"Come on back," Jefferson told the Malones.

Kyle and Lauren walked around Clyde's desk and made their way to the far right corner of the dingy office.

"Have a seat," Jefferson motioned the two iron folding chairs in front of him.

The couple sat down and Jefferson took his place behind a huge metal desk overflowing with files and papers.

"I'm sorry I missed you at the funeral yesterday," said Lauren. "I wanted to talk to you afterwards but I couldn't find you."

"Regrettably, I had to leave early. I had a shift," Jefferson responded. "I'm glad that you stopped by, though."

"Look Jefferson, this isn't exactly a social call," said Lauren lowering her voice. "We came to find out what's going on with Delmar's case."

"Well you know that I can't discuss an open case with you, Lauren."

"Come on Jefferson. How long have we known each other? We were all friends before you joined the police force," Lauren argued. "You have to tell us something!"

"We think that there is more to Delmar's death than just a robbery," Kyle said quietly, trying another tactic.

"What makes you say that?" Jefferson asked curiously.

"Well Delmar told Lauren some things a couple of weeks ago when he came to visit us in Macon. Something about the sold properties on the island."

Jefferson was silent for a moment. He knew something wasn't right about this case but he just didn't have a clue as to what. Jefferson motioned the couple forward. "What I have to tell you is between us. If anything gets back to my chief, it's my job."

"We'll put it on lock," Lauren assured Jefferson that his secret was safe.

"I think there is more going on also. First of all, Delmar was shot at very close range, meaning his assailant was most likely someone he knew. Secondly, there was something obviously missing from his wall but nothing of value was taken. Thirdly, his office was trashed in a way that makes me think that someone was looking for something."

"What are the police going to do? Do they have any suspects?"

"We've questioned the cleaning crew who found him – you remember the Rashads? The guys thought that maybe they were down on their luck and tried to rob Delmar, then shooting him when he didn't give them anything."

"I don't buy that," Lauren said fiercely shaking her head. "Carlos and Dee Rashad have cleaned those offices for years and they've never robbed anyone. Besides, they know our families. They wouldn't harm us."

"I agree and that's what I told them but you can't tell these newcomers about our ways. They just don't get it."

Lauren nodded in understanding the predicament. This was one reason the islanders had a huge distrust for outsiders.

"Anyway, if they can't hang this 'robbery' on the Rashads, the chief has been ordered to close the case."

"What?!" exclaimed Lauren rising to her feet.

"Baby, calm down," said Kyle gently placing his wife back into her chair. The rest of the cops in the large room looked around at her. Ignoring them, Kyle asked Jefferson in a lowered voice, "Ordered by whom?"

"Couldn't tell you," Jefferson said. "But from the sound of things, the order came from pretty high up."

"I'll just bet it did," Lauren grumbled. "That means our theory is right and this is about the sold properties."

"Don't worry, Lauren. I plan to find out what really happened to Delmar," said Jefferson. "That's a promise."

"Well you won't be by yourself because I won't rest until the truth is uncovered. So you better plan on us communicating quite often."

Chapter 9

"Lauren, please be careful," Kyle pleaded through the car window. He had to return to work in the morning so he and Justin were headed back to Macon. "Whatever Delmar stumbled onto, it was information someone didn't want him to have. I couldn't stand it if something happened to you."

"I will be careful," Lauren promised. "I just need to find the truth about happened to Delmar. I refuse to let these people call it a simple robbery and just leave it at that. That's insulting on so many levels."

"If I didn't have important meetings this week, I would stay here with you."

"I know but I'll be fine." She spied her toddler strapped into the back seat. "Bye-bye Justin. You listen to Daddy, okay?"

Justin's answers came in claps and laughter.

"Tell Mama, 'okay.'" Lauren prompted him.

"Okay," he answered obediently.

"The daycare center is expecting him this week," said Lauren. "You can drop him off on the way to work."

"Got it," Kyle said as if she hadn't mentioned the daycare at least five times in the past hour. He cut his wife some slack. She'd never been away from Justin for more than one night.

"Tell Mama, 'bye-bye.'" Kyle instructed Justin.

"Bye-bye, Mama."

"Bye-bye, Baby." Lauren blew him a kiss.

"Bye Lauren," said Kyle and kissed her. "Remember what I told you."

"I will," Lauren responded as Kyle backed out of the long driveway. "I'll be home soon."

When Kyle's car disappeared down the dusty road, she went back inside the house.

"You should have gone with them," said John as soon as she walked into the kitchen.

"Have I worn out my welcome already?" Lauren teased as she began to clear away the dishes left over from breakfast.

"You could never do that," John responded. "But I am worried about your safety."

"I'll be careful, Dad. Besides, I'll be working with Jefferson. He'll protect me."

"He'd better because I've already lost my nephew. I will not lose my daughter too."

Chapter 10

Lauren parked her mother's car in front of Delmar's office and tried to get up the courage to walk in. Jefferson told her that all the evidence had already been collected and it was okay for her to go in. She was having strong reservations against going into the last place where her cousin was seen alive. Gathering her courage, Lauren got out of the car, careful not to ding the door of the white SUV that pulled in next to her.

Lauren cautiously walked to the office of the building inspector and carefully turned the knob. The door opened easily. It was dark inside. Clara, the receptionist apparently hadn't returned to work since the murder. Lauren walked past the counter towards Delmar's office in back.

Lauren was not prepared for what she saw when she turned on the light. The office was beyond trashed. It seemed like every single piece of paper in Delmar's office had been thrown to the floor. His computer, brand new by the look of it, was also on the floor completely smashed. When Lauren caught a look at the blood stains, now brown, on the floor near her shoes, she collapsed to her knees in agony. When she finally regained her composure some fifteen minutes later, she had a more determined look to her face and she was set to walk away from Delmar's office with answers.

Lauren looked around, forcing herself to take everything in. Jefferson was right about something being missing from the wall. There were fliers and memos covering every inch of the wall except for a blank space that looked to be about 20 by 25 square inches. Upon closer look she could see strips of paper still stuck to the wall indicating that it had been ripped down. Lauren thought back to when she was working as a planner and what was usually posted on her own walls.

"It had to be a map," Lauren decided. "Whatever it was a map of, someone clearly didn't want anyone to see it posted on his wall."

Next Lauren went over to the open drawers of the file cabinet. They were empty, of course. Sifting through the papers strewn across the floor, she knew what she was looking for now. She continued searching until she was certain that she had covered every inch of the small office.

"That can't be possible," Lauren mumbled.

She searched the room again. She still didn't find what she was looking for. Lauren looked around one last time.

"All of the rezoning files for the past year are missing. So are all of the building permits. Someone is definitely trying to cover his tracks."

Chapter 11

"Hey, thanks for meeting me," Lauren pushed back her chair and gave Netta a hug.

"I know that we said that we would do lunch," Netta said as she said down. "But I admit that I was surprised when you called this morning and asked me to meet you at Duke's. I figured you would be back in Macon by now."

"I sent Kyle and Justin back this morning," said Lauren as she opened her menu. "But I decided to stay in Oak Grove a few more days."

"Catching up with the family?" Netta asked also opening her menu.

"No, just doing some sleuthing," Lauren replied casually. "What looks good?"

"It hasn't been that long since you've been to Duke's Café. It's all good," Netta told her. Then she asked, "What kind of sleuthing?"

Before Lauren could answer her, the waitress appeared.

"I'll have the fried chicken and collard greens," Lauren ordered.

"And for you?" the waitress asked Netta.

"I'll have the same and an extra side of coleslaw."

"Very good," said the waitress stuffing her order pad back into her apron pocket and sticking her pencil into her braided hair. "I'll put this order in then I'll be back to fill your glass. Sweet tea, right?"

"Can you bring me back a coke?" Netta asked.

"No problem," said the waitress and she walked off in the direction of the kitchen.

"I've always loved this restaurant," said Netta of the small mainland café. It was a small rustic place with wooden tables and benches that served as chairs as if they were on a picnic. The tables were covered with red and white checkered table clothes and each had a homemade doll center piece.

"Me too," Lauren agreed. "We got a great table."

The two of them gazed out of the large picture window that overlooked the Sweet Brush River. They could see the plush green of Oak Grove Island on the other side of the waterway.

"You never did tell me about that sleuthing you said you were doing," said Netta refusing to let go of the subject. "What are you up to?"

"Oh right," Lauren remembered. "It's about Delmar."

"What about Del?" Netta asked reaching for a hush puppy out of the basket that had been placed in the center of the table.

Lauren looked around to make sure she wasn't overheard. "I don't think he was killed in a failed robbery attempted." She spoke in almost a whisper. "I think he was killed for another reason."

"What?!" Netta exclaimed. "Did the police say something? Does Cousin Dinah know?"

"No, the police haven't said anything," Lauren responded, skirting the truth about Jefferson as she promised to protect his involvement with the case. "But –"

Just then, the waitress arrived with their drinks served in mason jars with lots of ice, and Lauren quieted immediately.

"Your food should be out in just a moment," she said laying two straws on the table.

"Thank you," said Lauren.

"Thank you," mumbled Netta, irritated that they were interrupted.

No sooner than the waitress left, Netta was on Lauren to finish her sentence.

"But what?" she prompted.

"I have my own theories. I think Delmar found out something about the sold properties in Oak Grove that someone didn't want him to know."

"And you're basing this on what?" Netta asked as she carefully sipped her coke.

"There were things missing from his office."

"Hello! Lauren!" Netta said exasperated. "Usually when someone is *robbed*, things turn up missing."

"No Netta. His files are missing. His computer had been smashed. If he were being robbed, why wouldn't they just take the computer? Why smash it to the ground?"

"Wait, how do you know what happened to his files and computer?"

"I went to his office this morning," Lauren confessed. "You should have seen it, Netta, it was horrible."

"Are you crazy?!" Netta hissed angrily. "Who do you think you are going there? Did you make a career change? Were you suddenly deputized and forgot to tell me about it?

"Netta, why are you so upset?" Lauren asked confused. She could understand worry but Netta sounded furious. "Don't you want to know what really happened to Delmar?"

"What do you mean what 'really' happened. He was robbed. He didn't give the robber what he wanted like the dumbass he could be sometimes and the robber shot him!"

"Netta!" Lauren gasped. "How could you say that about Delmar?"

"Why are you treating him like Saint Delmar?" Netta raised her voice. "You act like he could do nothing wrong. He was always such a know-it-all and look where that got him. Dead."

Lauren's light brown eyes met Netta's dark angry ones for a moment.

"So you're disregarding the reasons I gave you?" Lauren asked in an evenly toned voice. "You're going to accept this lame robbery theory and that's it? You sound like you think he had this coming."

"I just think that you're trying to start some mess, that's what I think," said Netta as the waitress brought out the food.

"I'm sorry you feel that way," said Lauren as the chicken was placed in front of her. Suddenly, it looked so unappetizing or maybe it was just the knot in that just formed in her stomach.

Lauren watched as Netta devoured her lunch as if they didn't just have an argument not even a minute ago. Their whole life their friendship ran hot and cold. One moment they were the best of friends, playing in the yard at each other's houses and passing notes in homeroom in school. The next moment, they wouldn't be speaking for some reason and Delmar would have to be the go-between and try to keep the peace.

Lauren cringed when she remembered how they used Delmar for the "tell-her-I-saids," such as "Delmar, tell Netta I said that she's an immature brat!" or "Delmar, tell Lauren I said, 'Your Mama!'"

"Tell-her-I-saids" could go on for days until one of them apologized (It was usually Lauren who apologized after a desperate urge from Delmar) or in an even rarer instance, they just simply forgot the reason they were angry at one another.

Lauren only picked at her food because in that one fleeting moment, she realized her exact relationship with Netta. At its very core, Delmar was the glue that held together Lauren and Netta. He was constant and unwavering in his love for both girls, now women. Now

Delmar was gone and so was the glue. There was no one there to say "Tell her I said". Now they would either have to be mature women and make up without the go-between or just simply go their separate ways. Lauren wondered if she would ever be able to retain a friendship with Netta now that there was only the two of them.

Chapter 12

Being on the mainland, Lauren thought this would be a good opportunity to go by Delmar's apartment. She didn't think that her aunt and uncle cleaned it out yet. Lauren knew Delmar's death was hard on them. She couldn't even imagine the strength that it would take to go through their son's personal belongings and shut it away in a box. Where does it all go anyway? In the attic? In a closet? Would his clothes go to Goodwill? What would happen to his car that was not yet paid for? Everything in Delmar's life seemed so unfinished. That's what happens when someone is taken away from this earth so suddenly.

Just like it was hard to go to Delmar's office, Lauren knew that it would be also hard, if not harder to go to his apartment. However, she was even more determined now particularly after the argument she had with Netta.

After saying goodbye to Netta, who only mumbled the reply before hopping into her old beat-up Camry and drove away, Lauren had gotten into her mother's car and drove south on Coastal Highway. She pulled into a complex of white Spanish styled apartments of two and three stories called *The Villas* and parked in front of Delmar's building. Lauren climbed the three flights of stairs and searched for the spare key in the potted palm by the door.

She felt a little funny about letting herself into her dead cousin's apartment. The good thing was that the front door was hidden from the view of the nosy neighbors. Lauren hesitantly pushed open the heavy oak door, which gave an ominous squeak. The slightly opened vertical blinds bathed the room with a natural light, revealing that once again, someone unwelcome had let himself in. Delmar's apartment, like his office was trashed. Lauren knew she should have left that instant and called Jefferson in case the intruder was still there, but her feet remained planted on the floor as she took in the dreadful scene. His books had been thrown from the shelves. Quite a few of them were broken at the spine. The potted plants were uprooted and the dirt strewn all over the floor. The sofa and the armchair had been slashed by a knife. The stuffing was still pouring out of the cushions. Pictures were smashed, the mirrors were cracked, and the phone had been ripped from the wall.

Robbery indeed! Lauren wanted to scream at Netta. Who in the hell would rob someone's home leaving the big flat screen plasma television, computer, and stereo smashed on the floor?

Lauren shook away the disbelief. She had things to do before the police were called. Shuffling her way through the debris towards Delmar's desk, she used a tissue to open his drawers as she'd seen them do on television as to not leave behind any of her fingerprints.

Lauren had hoped that whatever Delmar had at the office, he had copies of at home. Apparently, the murderer was on the same wavelength. The drawers were empty. No files, no computer disks, nothing. Whoever came in here knew what they were doing.

Lauren sighed in frustration. She turned to leave and had already opened the door before deciding to check Delmar's bedroom for any clues. She closed the front door back and walked a couple of steps when she felt the crunch of glass beneath her feet. Looking down, she saw that it was a picture of Delmar, Netta, and her when they were about 12. Their smiling faces were pressed together looking like the happiest children in the world.

Granddad Lazarus had taken this picture, Lauren remembered. Her parents had the same picture pressed into their photo album back at the house but it had been a while since Lauren had seen it.

Granddad had allowed them to go with him to the farmer's market on the mainland to sell the fruits and vegetables he'd harvested. Lauren remembered how the three of them were piled in the back of Granddad's 1968 blue Volkswagen van among the watermelon, cucumbers, tomatoes, and peaches, with the air blowing in from the rolled down windows, whipping against their eager faces.

After they sold their produce at the market, the four of them had a picnic lunch on a grassy spot by the river.

They could see the plush green foliage in the distance that was Oak Grove Island.

"Granddad, how long have you lived on Oak Grove Island?" Delmar had asked as he grabbed a crispy chicken thigh from the plastic Tupperware bowl.

"I was born there, just like you all were," was Granddad's answer before taking a bite from his own piece of chicken.

Then Lauren asked, "How long has our family been here?"

Granddad swallowed his food and said, "Since the Civil War."

"Nah-uh!" Netta had exclaimed with disbelief almost spilling her lunch on the picnic blanket.

"Oh yes" Granddad had insisted right back and took a swig from his can of *Nihi* Grape soda.

"Really?" asked Lauren impressed.

"I'll tell you just as my granddad told it to me. It was late one night near the end of the Civil War – You learned about the Civil War during your studies?"

"Yessir!" Delmar had answered quickly. "That was the war that gave the slaves their freedom!"

Delmar had always been good in school.

"How right you are!" Granddad had responded proud of his grandson. "When was it fought?"

"1850," had been Netta's answer.

"Nope! But you're close."

"1860-1864," Lauren spoke up. Fascinated by this story, her own food sat untouched on her paper plate.

"That's right. You're smart kids," Granddad had said. "So it was towards the end of the war in 1864 and the fighting was getting close, so close in fact that the sound of those cannons would make the ground shake. All of the slaves, that included those coming from the LaCrosse Plantation, decided that they needed to flee, lest they get caught up in the fighting."

"The LaCrosse Plantation?" Lauren questioned with her eyes stretched wide.

"Yes, don't you know slaves took on the names of their owners?"

"No, I didn't," she'd replied shaking her head.

"Well they did. That's how we ended up with the name. We were owned by the LaCrosses, a white family that had a plantation off the mainland a few miles north of here, so I was told."

"Can we see it?" Delmar had asked.

"What you wanna see it for?" Netta had asked him crossly. In fact, she'd been sullen since Granddad told her that her answer was incorrect. History had never been her best subject.

"Netta, it's a part of our history," was Delmar's patient explanation. "Don't you want to see where we all came from?"

"Not really," declared Netta and began to crunch on her potato chips loudly.

"I believe the plantation burned in the war. The family lost track of its exact location," Granddad had continued, interrupting a potential argument between his grandson and grandniece. "Anyway, as I was saying, the slaves gathered up their family and the bare necessities and headed east towards the river."

"What about their owners, what would have happened if they found out?" Lauren had asked breathlessly.

"All the men had left to fight in the war. There was only womenfolk on the plantation, so there was no one left to chase them."

"That's pretty chauvinistic, Granddad," Lauren told him.

Lazarus laughed and rubbed Lauren's braided head. "I'm just telling you how it was, Sweetheart. So at the risk of being called a *chauvinist*, the women of the big house were too busy saving their fine things rather than to worry about a few ole slaves, so they took their opportunity and slipped out late one night.

They walked for miles making their way through the trees and underbrush. It was very important that they did this quickly and quietly. Who knew what would happen if they were caught."

"Why, what could happen?" had been Netta's question. She too was getting caught up in the story in spite of herself.

"There was no telling during those uncertain times. They might have been taken back to the plantation. Or they could have possibly been killed if found by the wrong people."

"Like who?"

"Confederate soldiers maybe or some poor farmer struggling to keep his way of life, I would imagine. But that's just speculation. One thing for certain, they didn't want to go back to the plantation."

"So did they make it?" asked Lauren.

"Of course they made it, Lor," Delmar had responded with a smirk. "Or we wouldn't be here."

"What I meant to say is did they *all* make it?" Lauren restated her question as she cut her eyes at Delmar.

"Yeah, sure you did," Delmar teased.

"Let me finish the story, now," Granddad had said. "It was a couple of hours before dawn when they arrived at the waterside. In fact, it was about here where we're sitting."

"Here?" The three had jumped up as if they'd been bitten. To be standing in the actual footsteps of their ancestors was a powerful thing.

"Yes children, here. They had to swim over. Water carries sound so they kept the babies quiet by stuffing cotton into their mouths."

The three children had looked out at the water to the land that was Oak Grove Island. It wasn't far if traveling by car across the bridge, but to swim a couple of miles carrying babies and belongings must have been a difficult experience.

They were all silent for a few moments as if to honor their memories.

"Do you know where the slaves ended up?" asked Granddad finally breaking the silence.

"There?" Delmar had asked pointing across the creek.

"Yes and where is there?"

The three cousins exchanged confused glances. It was Oak Grove Island, that's all they knew.

"That's LaCrosse property. To be exact, that's your grandparents' land, Netta. In fact, the house should be on the other side of that cluster of palmettos over there."

"My granddad and grandma? We can see their land from here?"

"That's right."

"That's so cool." Delmar had been impressed.

"It sure is," Lauren had agreed.

"When the war was over, we were allowed to keep that land that the slaves settled."

"Are there more islands like this, Granddad?" Lauren had asked. "Where the slaves settled?"

"From Florida to North Carolina."

"Wow…"

"So now that you know your history and how we came by this land, I am going to charge you three with some very important instructions, as my oldest grandchildren – and grandniece."

"I have an older sister, Uncle" Netta had reminded him.

"That's okay," Granddad Lazarus had said to her. "She's not here, so I am giving *you* this responsibly.

"What do you want us to do, Granddad?" Delmar had asked.

"It's not what I want you to do. It's what I *don't* want you to do."

"Okay, what *don't* you want us to do?"

"I don't ever want you sell the LaCrosse land. The land is the only thing we black folks have to call our own. Down on them southern islands, black folks are selling properties to these white developers for chump change.

Now some didn't realize what they had before they sold it. The white folks got it now and they're putting up these golf courses, condos, and beach front houses. They're making these places their own personal playground. The property taxes go up and folks can't afford to keep their land so they also lose it."

"Granddad, how do you know that the same thing won't happen on Oak Grove Island?" Delmar had asked.

"It won't if black folks hold together and not sell their land. That way we can keep this island for ourselves. But no matter what happens with the other families, I want the three of you to promise me that you won't sell the LaCrosse land."

"We promise," the three vowed.

Lauren was swiftly brought back to the present by a sound in the bedroom. Scared out of her wits, she grabbed her purse, breaking the shoulder strap and ran for the door. She flew down the three flights of stairs taking them two at a time until she hit the bottom, fumbling for her keys all the while. Lauren's hands violently shook but she managed to get the key in the ignition. She thrust the gear shift in reverse backing out of the parking space. She barely stopped the car before quickly shifting into drive and tearing out of complex narrowly missing an oncoming car.

Lauren checked her rear view mirror. As far as she could tell, no one was following her. She was on the bridge to Oak Grove Island before reaching in her purse for her cell phone.

"Ouch," Lauren cut her finger on something but she wasn't concerned about what it was at the moment.

Finding her cell, Lauren quickly located Jefferson's number.

"Hey Lauren, what's going on?"

"Jefferson quick! Send some units to Delmar's apartment. It's completely trashed and I think whoever did it is still there."

"Lauren, where are you?"

"I'm just getting off the bridge."

"Are you being followed?"

Lauren checked her mirror again. "No."

"Alright, listen to me. Go home and stay there. I'll be in touch."

Lauren hung up. For the first time since she ran out of Delmar's apartment, she could fully appreciate the situation. For all she knew Delmar's killer could be in his apartment and she could have been next. Lauren decided to keep what happened from Kyle and her parents. From this point forward, she would have to be more careful.

Chapter 13

"Did you get him?" Lauren asked after she opened the front door to let Jefferson in a couple of hours later.

Jefferson walked into the family room with Lauren at her heels.

"No, he was gone when we got there," he replied not looking at her. "You must have scared him away."

"Man! This guy seems to always be one step ahead!"

Jefferson looked around the room. "Are your parents here?"

"Yeah, they're upstairs in their room. Do you want me to get them?"

"No," said Jefferson closing the doors to the family room. "I just don't want them to overhear me yelling at you. Do you realize what a sticky situation you almost gotten yourself into?"

"Believe me, I know," Lauren answered.

"No you don't know!" Jefferson snapped. "So I'll break it down for you. The intruder broke in through the bedroom window."

"I didn't know that."

"He could have been there the entire time you were there."

"I already figured that out, Jeff," said Lauren testily. "But if he wanted to hurt me, he had plenty of opportunity."

"That just makes you lucky!" Jefferson snapped. "Lauren, what on earth possessed you to go to Delmar's apartment?!"

"I was looking for clues."

"Oh really? Well I think you need to go back to Macon and let me do the investigating."

"Yeah right. I bet you would love that. So what are your colleagues saying? Do they still think it's a robbery?"

Jefferson just looked away.

"Well do they?!"

"They want to bring the Rashads back in for questioning," Jefferson said in a lowered voice.

"Ha! So in other words, they still think that Delmar was robbed."

"Yes."

"Well I'm not going anywhere then because as you can see, I still have work to do."

"Let me do it, Lauren. It's my job."

"Okay then," Lauren said with mock patience. "Whatcha got?"

"Um...well it wasn't a robbery," Jefferson offered feebly.

"Uh, we've already established that. Tell me something I don't know," said Lauren folding her arms impatiently.

Jefferson was silent again.

"You can't? Okay, then I'll tell you what *I've* got. Did you know that all of the rezoning files and building permits are missing for the past year?"

"No."

"Yes, they are. I'm thinking that there is something in those files that someone does not want us to see and it has something to do with the sold properties around the island. Do you know what's missing from Delmar's office wall?"

"No."

"Bet you a year's salary that it was a map. All planners have maps on their walls."

"Planner? I thought Del was a building inspector."

"He's both. It's just that in small towns the two are synonymous. In some places, the building inspector doesn't know squat about rezonings although they're required to make those types of recommendations. But Delmar actually had a Masters in Urban Planning."

"I didn't know that," Jefferson said softly. "What was on the map, do you know?"

"His map was most likely a map of Oak Grove, either a zoning map or a future land use map. Whatever it was, we need to find out what was on it because it's a clue."

"To the sold properties?"

"Now you're catching on."

"So why go to Delmar's apartment."

"Because I was hoping to find copies of the missing records there. So while you and your police officers were checking out forced entries and speculating robberies, did you notice that his files and computer disks are missing also?"

"No."

"And that Jefferson, is why you need me here," said Lauren. "You don't know what you're looking for but I do. Kyle and I *Googled* the Wessler-Forrest Corporation."

"Who?"

"See, you're further making my point. Wessler-Forrest is the name on the signs mounted on the sold properties. They mainly specialize in large scaled development such as condos, golf courses, exclusive shops, and subdivisions. If these Wessler people are coming here buying up property, there had to have been a whole lot of rezonings going through council."

"How do you know all of this?" Jefferson asked amazed.

"Because I also have a Masters in Urban Planning." Lauren let that sink in for a moment before she continued.

"Look, a lot of the properties on the island are zoned *Agricultural* based on the present land use. You can't put this type of large scale development on land with an *Agricultural* classification. It would need to be changed to one that supports a higher density development such as commercial, mixed use, or high density residential."

"Okay, I need you," Jefferson relented. "But from now on you are no longer investigating on your own. You take me with you."

"Fine. How do you feel about going with me to the tax accessor's office tomorrow morning?"

"What do you need there?"

"Since we don't have Delmar's files, I need another way to find out how much property these Wessler-Forrest people have acquired."

"Okay."

"Also, if you'll get the minutes from the planning commission and the town council meetings, that will tell us exactly how many rezonings have actually gone through and other specifics."

"Okay, where do I get those?"

"The town clerk should get you everything you need."

"Wait a minute, who's running this investigation?" Jefferson asked suddenly confused with his role.

"With all of the information that I've just given you, do you even have to ask?"

Chapter 14

"I need the tax maps for 2004 through 2005 and 2005 through 2006, please," Lauren asked the clerk. She and Jefferson had traveled thirty miles to the county tax office with the hopes that they could get that much closer to solving the mystery of Delmar's death.

"They're over there," the clerk drawled pointing a crimson nail at a bookshelf by the wall.

"Thank you. How much to make copies?"

"Twenty-five cents a page."

"Thank you." Then she said to Jefferson, "Let's get to work."

"This property is not for sale," Lauren could hear her father's voice as she and Jefferson entered through the front door.

"I can make it worth your while," said a tall, thin, blonde man who looked to be in his early twenties. He was sitting on the edge of the seat in one of the armchairs in the livingroom with an open briefcase on the coffee table.

"You can't offer me any amount of money that will make me sell this property," John said refusing the card the man offered him.

The man closed his briefcase, rose to his feet, and left his card on the coffee table anyway. "If you change your mind, give me a call."

"You forgot your card," said John pointing to the coffee table.

"Keep it," said the man walking past Lauren and Jefferson. He opened the front door, turned back to them and said, "Just in case."

Lauren slammed the front door closed as soon as he walked out.

"Who was that, Daddy?" Lauren demanded to know.

"That was a man who is under the mistaken impression that our property is for sale." John snatched the card off the coffee table and crumpled it up before tossing it in the trash in the kitchen. He grabbed his keys off the counter and headed out the back door.

Lauren reached into the trash and retrieved the card. It read Bryce Wessler, CEO, Wessler-Forrest Corporation.

"So this is Bryce Wessler," she said recognizing his name from the company website. She studied his picture.

The cold ice-blue eyes stared back at her. "Man these corporate bigwigs get younger and younger."

She put the card in her front pocket and headed for the family room with Jefferson on her heels.

They spent three hours flipping through copies of tax records and highlighting the properties that changed owners over the past two years.

"Are you seeing what I am seeing?" Lauren asked observing the documents very closely.

"I see that a lot of the properties have been acquired by the Wessler-Forrest Corporation."

"One third to be exact," Lauren told him as she highlighted a map of Oak Grove Island.

When she was finished highlighting, she held up the map for Jefferson to see. "The corporation had taken over the entire center of the island."

"Wow," Jefferson breathed. "That's a lot of acres."

Then Lauren gave him the bad news. "These highlighted acres are only what's been recorded so far. There's no telling how many properties have yet to be updated on the tax records."

"I don't even want to think about it," Jefferson groaned. "Look, the yellow is spreading towards Creekside."

"They've already started on Creekside," said Lauren pulling out Wessler's card and holding it out for Jefferson to see.

"I wonder if they've gotten to my parents' house yet. It's just up the road."

"Judging by the direction of the yellow," said Lauren studying the tax map. "It's just a matter of time."

Chapter 15

"The maps shows that they've got the Perry and Clarkson Communities, so they've got a good number of properties along the Blue Creek," Lauren was speaking to Kyle over the phone giving her nightly updates on the progress of the investigation.

"So they've started with the center of the island," Kyle was saying in disbelief. "I'm surprised that they hadn't started with the beachfront properties."

"They probably have but my grandmother owns most of the beachfront property, which is about 500 acres. She's not about to part with that."

"I knew it was a lot, but I didn't know it was that much."

"Yes it is, and Aunt Eleanor owns the 500 on the riverside, so fortunately, that's safe also."

"Wow," Kyle admonished. "If developers ever got a hold of those properties, it would be all over for Oak Grove. Those are prime spots. Developers would have a field day."

"Don't worry," said Lauren remembering the pact that she, Delmar, and Netta made with Lazarus. "They're not getting the LaCrosse land."

"And so they approached your dad today?" Kyle asked in disbelief.

"Yes they did. And Jefferson and Delmar's parents also, as well as a few other families that live in Creekside. Fortunately, they refused to sell. If they had, the developers would get the rest of Blue Creek."

"I always wondered how your parents and Delmar's parents ended up with their own separate property on the other side of the island."

"Granddad Lazarus," said Lauren. "He thought that land was very important to have. He would give his sons a piece of his land, of course, but when these lots along the creek came up for sale, Granddad encouraged our dads to buy the properties while they were still cheap."

"That was smart," Kyle commented. Then he said, "Lor, I can be back on the island this weekend."

"With Justin?"

"I figure we can leave him with Nate and Angel. With all of your investing, I don't think it would be safe for him."

"Good idea," said Lauren. "Justin will enjoy staying with his Godparents."

"Hey look, while I got you on the phone, I think I got a lead on a job for you," said Kyle.

"Oh really?" Lauren asked suddenly excited. "Where?"

"One of my clients who's working on that downtown project with us, has a planner friend who is moving back to Oregon. She's leaving behind a position at the Macon Area Planning Center."

"What do they do?"

"Mostly regional planning, I believe. Land use planning is their biggest thing."

"Is it advertised?" Lauren asked. She checked the planning web pages daily and didn't remember seeing that position.

"Not yet, but my client said that he would talk to her for you and see if you can get an interview. Is your resume still on the computer?"

"Yes, it's on the desk top," said Lauren. "That would be really great if I could get this job. I've been so anxious to get back into planning again. And you know I've always wanted to do comprehensive land use planning."

"That's what I told him," said Kyle. "I'll pass along your resume to him."

"It's great to have people in high places," Lauren teased.

"You know I'm always looking out!" Said Kyle. "So I'll see you in a couple of days."

"I'll be here."

"Be safe."

Chapter 16

"You want to bring the Rashads in for suspicion of murder?! Based on what?!" Lauren overhead Jefferson confronting the police chief when she arrived at the police station the next morning.

"Based on the fact that they do not have an acceptable alibi for the break-in of Delmar LaCrosse's apartment. They had means and opportunity to attack LaCrosse in his office."

"We haven't even recovered the murder weapon," Jefferson protested.

"We're dragging the creek for it now."

"Which creek?"

"Look Jefferson, do I have to remove you from this case?"

"No sir!" Jefferson replied firmly.

"Good because I need you. Now I want the Rashads brought in, booked and fingerprinted. Send a couple of the boys out if you don't feel comfortable doing it yourself." Those were the chief's final words before walking away.

As Lauren approached Jefferson tentatively, she heard him mumble, "Oh I'm going to bring someone in alright, but it won't be the Rashads."

"Hey Jefferson," Lauren spoke up.

"Hey Lauren. Didn't see you there. Look, I've got some bad news for you," said Jefferson as he fumbled through the papers on his desk to find his car keys.

"I heard. You're bringing in the Rashads for Delmar's murder."

"Yeah, that's right, but that's not what I meant. I went by the town clerk's office to ask for the minutes for the planning commission and town council meetings and they don't have them."

"What do you mean they don't have them?" Lauren asked indignantly. "How can they not keep minutes? They're supposed to have a public record of everything that goes on in those meetings"

"They do have them but what I mean to say is that they aren't exactly up to date."

"How far behind are they?" Lauren asked fearing the answer.

Jefferson confirmed her fear. "A little over a year."

"Are you kidding me?" Lauren exclaimed.

"See the way that it was explained to me is that Edgie Ashcome, who used to take the short hand and then type them up, left to go to accounting school."

"Over a year ago," Lauren guessed dryly.

"Right. They hadn't been able to find someone qualified ever since so every meeting, each council member takes a turn turning on the tape recorder and another member does the typing of the minutes. The whole plan fell apart the first town council meeting. They would turn on the tape recorder but a fight erupted over whose turn it was to do the typing because no one wanted to do it and now it's big mess. Now they just turn the tape recorder on and don't worry too much about typing up the minutes."

"So who keeps the tapes of the minutes, maybe I can listen to them," Lauren asked feeling that maybe all hope wasn't lost.

"The clerk told me that the tapes are dispersed among the different council members. They were never all that pressed about keeping them in one place."

"Oh Lord," Lauren groaned. She took in a deep breath and blew it out of her mouth slowly. "So um, so what do they approve at the meetings every month?"

"They don't."

"How can they not? Is that even legal?"

"This is Oak Grove. Barely anything goes on here. There's barely a reason to keep minutes and up until now, no one has even asked for them."

"Jefferson, maybe a year ago that was true. Now with all of these rezonings going through, more is going to start happening and there is going to be a need for better record keeping. If this isn't taken seriously immediately, the island is asking for trouble."

"I know you're right but what can we do?" Jefferson sighed. "So where does this lead us with the investigation?"

Lauren smoothed her thick hair away from her face then said, "Back to the beginning."

Chapter 17

Lauren sat behind the wheel of her mother's car and thought about her next steps. She was just going to have to figure this out without the council minutes. Based on the tax maps, she knew what properties had been bought, but the minutes would have told her if the rezonings on those properties had actually passed. Without Delmar's files or the council minutes, she didn't know where else to look. The town didn't even have a website so that option was out. The rezonings Lauren knew, were the key to finding out the reason for Delmar's murder.

Lauren started the car after deciding to head to Beachside on the other side of the island. Since she was stumped for now, she thought she would pay Grandma Henrietta a visit. Besides, it wouldn't hurt to see if she had been contacted by those developers also.

As Lauren made the dusty drive to the north side of the island, the exterior thermometer on the car read 95 degrees. It felt hotter than that so when she spotted the general store coming up on the right, Lauren pulled into the small lot out in front and hopped out. She was busy trying to decide which flavor of Poweraid she wanted and almost didn't hear someone call out her name.

"Aunt Eleanor!" Lauren spoke with enthusiasm to the heavy-set elderly woman sitting in the backseat of an old beat up blue Camry with all of the windows rolled down. Netta's Camry. "What are you doing sitting out here in the heat?"

Aunt Eleanor was dressed in her lilac and white flowered "goin'-to-town dress," soaked through with perspiration. Wearing her usual mean expression on her face, she was using her matching lilac hat as a fan, but the sweat was still pouring down her face. Her hair, which had been carefully curled that morning, was starting to droop in the mid-90 degree weather, giving another reason to further cloud her already sour disposition.

"Ask my granddaughter," she responded narrowing her already tight dark eyes, which made her look even meaner. "She and that no count husband of hers drove me down to the doctor this morning but they just had to stop on the way home to pick up a few things. I can't move too good on a count of my knee, so I'm sittin' here."

"Why didn't they just leave the car on so you could run the air conditioning?" Lauren questioned.

"'Cause they ain't wanna run the gas down with it being as high as it is. Netta ain't movin' too many of them houses on the mainland so they can't afford to waste it,"

Aunt Eleanor answered as her fanning grew more vigorous. "See, this is why I need a license. If I'da drove myself, I'da been home by now! Just hope that hussy remembers my arthritis cream."

Lauren didn't even want to get in the middle of that. Aunt Eleanor had been putting Netta down ever since she had to take her and her sisters in to live.

Instead she said, "I hope you're well. Sorry I didn't get a chance to talk to you much this visit."

"I'm fine. Just my arthritis actin' up," said Aunt Eleanor who had put down the hat and was now dabbing her moist cleavage with a lace handkerchief. "Figured you woulda been back in Georgia by now."

"No, I wanted to stay a while and visit my parents," said Lauren, not really feeling comfortable to confiding her true reason to her great aunt.

"Oh so you ain't here to investigate Delmar's death like you some Barney Fife or somethin'."

Lauren was silent. She wondered how Aunt Eleanor knew that.

"Oh yeah, Netta told me that you said something about Delmar finding out some stuff about people's land or something like that."

Again Lauren was surprised. Netta never confided anything in her grandmother before. She didn't even tell her when she'd started her period. What made Netta tell her grandmother this?

"I just don't buy that it was a robbery, that's all," Lauren said not confirming the truth. "I just want to make sure the police are covering their basis."

88

"If people want to sell their property, that's their right, Lauren," Aunt Eleanor told her.

"Really? Is that what you plan to do?" asked Lauren looking her aunt in the eye.

"Girl, you takin' a tone, ain't ya? Get a husband, go off to Macon and think you grown!"

Suppressing the urge to roll her eyes, Lauren turned towards the store. "I need to go, Aunt Eleanor."

"You see Netta in there, tell her to hurry it up, now. A few more minutes in this hot car an' I'ma be a puddle now..."

"Bye Aunt Eleanor," said Lauren already walking towards the store. She could only take her great aunt in small doses, and today she seemed to use it up faster than usual.

Lauren walked across the old wooden porch and pulled the screen door open, almost bumping into Derek Skinner, Netta's husband. The rugged-looking, rough neck was an ex-con who did hard time for selling drugs. He spent his days pumping iron, so bumping into him was like bumping into a brick wall.

"Lauren!" Girl, you doin' alright?"

"Hey Derek," was Lauren's winded response as she tried not to look too closely at the wide jagged scar that ran from the edge of his right eye to his cheekbone, another souvenir from prison. "How are you?"

"I'm good," he broke into a grin, which oddly enough softened out his rough features. "I s'pose you came here for Delmar's funeral. That's a shame what happened to him. Good guy."

"Yeah it was," Lauren answered, not wanting to dwell on it too much.

"Netta's here, I know she gonna wanna say, hi." Before Lauren could stop him, Derek called out, "Hey Netta! Come say 'hey' to Lauren!"

Netta looked right at Lauren and went back to what she was doing.

"Don't mind her," Derek said to Lauren. "She always trippin' over somethin'. Good to see you but I'd better get back to the car before Granny has a fit."

"Yeah," Lauren said absently. "She said something about turning into a puddle."

Derek laughed. "See ya now," he said and headed for the door.

Lauren looked over at Netta who was giving her the cold shoulder and sighed. *Delmar's gone. There are no more 'Tell her I saids,'* She thought. *We either need to act like adults or move on our separate ways.*

Chapter 18

"Grandma, how are you?" Lauren greeted Henrietta when she opened the screened door.

"Fine, just fine," Grandma opened her arms. "Come give me a hug."

Henrietta was a thin woman who was about the same height as her granddaughter. Her kind face was the shade of mahogany that held very few lines in spite of her age. There was usually a smile in her dark brown eyes, but today they looked understandably sad. Losing Delmar had been hard on her and it showed in how tightly she grasped her oldest granddaughter. Lauren held onto her small frame taking in her scent of soap and fresh air. After letting go, she followed Grandma into the small house and the two sat down on the peach flowered sofa in the living room.

"How long are you here for?" Grandma asked.

In her mind Lauren thought, *As long as it takes to find Delmar's killer*, but she didn't want to worry Grandma. Instead she told her that she was there for a few more days.

"I'm glad. Your parents are probably glad to have you home, especially now," Henrietta said solemnly.

"I imagine that they are," Lauren responded gently.

"Yes, sometimes God calls his children home early," she said absently. "Only He knows why and it's not for us to question. Yes sir, God calls His children home early sometimes…"

"I know," said Lauren with a tear slipping down her cheek in spite of herself. "I still miss him though."

" 'Course you do. I do too. It's gonna be okay though."

The two sat quietly listening to the waves crashing roughly against the shore.

"That sounds so peaceful," Lauren commented. "I remember when the three of us used to sleep out on the screen porch. Those waves would always put me to sleep."

"You, Delmar, and Netta spent a lot of time on that porch. I've never seen three closer cousins," said Grandma.

"Yes we were close," Lauren said absently thinking about her recent argument with Netta at the restaurant and the snub earlier at the general store.

As if she could read her mind, Grandma asked, "How are you and Netta getting along these days?"

Lauren looked at her grandmother with amazement before she answered," Not so well."

"Figured as much," Grandma replied with a wise twinkle in her eye.

"But how did you know that?"

"Grandmama knows, Honey," she said chuckling. "You girls could never get along when it's just the two of you. You both were always so competitive. Netta was jealous of you because you got parents with good sense. You were jealous of Netta because she was always so popular in school. Delmar just took what life handed him and lived well. He didn't get hung up on the petty stuff."

Lauren was amazed at how much insight her grandmother had into her relationships with Netta and Delmar. "You're right, Grandma. Netta and I bump heads constantly because we're too busy wanting what the other has and not acknowledging the fact that we both have it pretty good. Life is too short and we are too old to be giving each other the silent treatment."

"So, what are you fighting about now?" Grandma fussed at Lauren.

Lauren sighed and decided to tell her grandmother the truth. "We're fighting about Delmar's death. I just don't think it was a robbery."

"Why do you think he was killed?" Grandma asked quietly, looking down at her hands that were in her lap.

"I think Delmar died because he found out something about all those sold properties on the island. Something someone didn't want him to know."

Henrietta was quiet for a moment. Then she took her strong hands and put them each on Lauren's cheeks. "Lauren. Baby, promise me that you will let the police find Delmar's killer."

Instead of giving her promise, Lauren asked, "Grandma, do you know something?"

Grandma let her go and looked away. "What would I know, Baby?"

"Grandma, did the developers come about this property?" Lauren asked steering the conversation away from the subject of Delmar's killer. Lauren wanted as much as possible to avoid making a promise to her grandmother that she knew she couldn't keep.

"They came," Grandma said. "But don't you worry. Them fool developers ain't gettin' this property. If they get everything else, there's nothing I can do about it. But when your Granddaddy Lazarus, God rest his soul, came and got me off that sugar plantation down in Louisiana some sixty years ago, he promised me I wouldn't have to work nobody's land but our own. I didn't believe him though. Negroes owning their own land was unheard of to me. Then Lazarus married me and brought me to this green land of beaches and palmettos trees and it was then that I knew that he was speaking the truth. I knew we had a treasure that most only dream of and it's going to stay ours. We're going to have something to pass onto our kids and grandkids."

Chapter 19

Lauren, back in her mother's car made the left turn onto Spanish Moss Road. No sooner than she made the turn, a white SUV was hot on her tail. Lauren moved over to let the SUV pass, but it remained right on her bumper. In a panic, Lauren mashed the accelerator and the Lexus LS went flying down the dirt road. She had to be careful because the last thing is needed was to fish tail on an unpaved road, lose control, and end up in a drainage ditch, which lined either side of the island roads. Fortunately, there hadn't been any rain or else mud puddles would have been an added worry.

Thump! The SUV rammed the back of Lauren's car. She held on tightly to the wheel to avoid swerving, and then she picked up speed. She was up to 80 miles per hour. She couldn't keep up this speed for too long because the road had sharp curves up ahead. If the driver of the white SUV knew this, he didn't care because he kept right on Lauren's tail. When Lauren swerved to the left, the SUV served to the left. When Lauren swerved to the right, then the SUV swerved to the right.

Lauren was afraid to reach for her cellphone or else risk losing control of her car. The first sharp curve came up ahead. Lauren wasn't crazy to take it at 85 miles an hour, so she slammed on the brakes, causing the SUV to hit her again, and then took the curve. Miraculously, Lauren kept control of the car. They came to the second curve and again Lauren maintained control. Unfortunately, the SUV stayed with her as if it had super glued itself to the Lexus during that last hit.

The road thankfully straightened out again and that's when it happened: The SUV came around on the left side and forced Lauren off the road and into the ditch on the right side of the road. The airbag painfully hit Lauren in the face, cushioning her from the steering wheel. The SUV screeched to a halt a few feet ahead.

Dazed, Lauren sat up slowly to find her legs pinned under the dashboard. She peered out of the cracked windshield to see the driver's door to the SUV swing open. Lauren's purse that held her cellphone had been thrown in that space between the passenger seat and the door and she couldn't reach it. Frantically looking around for a weapon, Lauren spied an umbrella with a sharp point behind the passenger seat. She stretched as far as she could, just reaching the handle with her fingertips. With a fierce determination, Lauren stretched herself as far as she could. Her hand finally closed around the umbrella with her mind set on the fact that she would get in a few hits on her assailant before she was shot. Maybe she could knock the gun out of his hand, assuming there was a gun.

Lauren waited with tense anticipation. The passenger door suddenly swung open and Lauren screamed as she swung her weapon.

"Hello!"

"Oh!" Lauren cried with surprise. "I'm so sorry!"

Staring at her through the passenger door was Mr. Clive Green, a faded overall clad gentleman in his 70s, who owned property up the road. Lauren was deeply relieved that it was Mr. Green and not a cold-blooded killer.

"You 'bout to take someone's head off ain't ya? Good thing yo' aim ain't that good."

"Sorry, Mr. Green, I thought…" Lauren looked out of the windshield to find the white SUV gone. "Nevermind, I'm just glad you found me."

"Hey, you John LaCrosse's daughter, ain't you?"

"Yes! Yes I am!"

"Are you hurt?" asked Mr. Green.

"I'm okay, but my legs are pinned."

"How did this happen? You take the curve too fast?"

"Um yeah, I guess I did," Lauren admitted. She decided that she had better not tell Mr. Green about the SUV.

"See, I say it time and time again: Womenfolk don't need to be drivin'!" he said and began to dial his cellphone. "That's a shame too. You done tore up this pretty car."

Chapter 20

"Hey man, what's going on," said Kyle letting Jefferson into the house. The two men headed for the family room where Lauren was resting comfortably with her right foot propped on the ottoman.

A sprained knee was the only injury Lauren sustained in an accident that could have been so much worse. She'd been worried about the damage to her mother's car and was afraid of her parents' reaction to her running off the road, which was *all* she told them.

Marne was just relieved that Lauren wasn't seriously hurt. John was quiet when Lauren relayed the story from a bed in the emergency room of the mainland hospital, but he too was relieved. He simply kissed his daughter on the forehead and left the curtained area to make a phone call.

"Okay, so here's the thing, Lauren didn't get a plate number so we're going to have to check out all of the SUVs matching the description," said Jefferson after he sat down. "We've got an old system so it's going to take some time to compile all of the late model white Ford Explorers in the county. Then we'll have to go through them and sort out which ones are registered in Oak Grove."

"That's assuming that the person who was chasing you is local," added Kyle. "You might need to face up to the possibility that we're dealing with an out-of-state maniac."

"Kyle is right," Jefferson agreed. "And if that's the case, it will be that much more difficult to nail down the driver."

"You mean we might never find out who it was that ran me off the road?" Lauren asked with alarm.

"One step at a time, let's not get ahead of ourselves," said Jefferson calmly. "First, we'll investigate to see what we can find locally. If nothing turns up then we'll consider other options."

"Okay fine," Lauren agreed.

"Did you really have to arrest the Rashads?" Kyle asked Jefferson, changing the subject.

"Unfortunately and based on some flimsy evidence, I might add," Jefferson rubbed his shaved head in frustration. "The folks aren't too happy with me about it either."

"It's not your fault," Kyle told him. "You were just doing your job."

"I appreciate you saying that. Folks don't see it that way, though."

"They're in jail right now?" asked Lauren.

"Yes. Their arraignment is tomorrow morning. With a murder rap, I doubt they'd make bail if bail is even set."

"This is terrible," Lauren groaned. "Those people are in their 60s. They don't need to be in jail for a crime they didn't commit."

"That's all the more reason to find the real killer," said Kyle.

Jefferson shuffled through a stack of papers. "The other thing I came to see you about is this." He handed Lauren the papers.

"What's this?" Lauren asked curiously as she carefully flipped through the stack.

"This is from my cousin, Marva who works in Telly Whitman's office."

"Who's Telly Whitman?" asked Kyle.

"He holds the Town Council seat for the south side of the island," Lauren answered. "He's the only non-native on the council."

"That's right," said Jefferson. "Marva was picking up a file off of Whitman's desk and accidentally picked up those papers for the new development the Wessler-Forrest Corporation is proposing."

"Oh my gosh!" Lauren exclaimed as she continued to read through the pages. "This is really valuable."

"Marva didn't fully understand what she stumbled across, but she did see that something wasn't right and made colored copies. Then she put the originals back on Whitman's desk."

"Kyle look!" Lauren exclaimed as she unfolded a huge document. "It's Oak Grove Island but not as we know it."

Kyle came around to one side of Lauren and Jefferson to the other.

"There's planned residential subdivisions with golf courses, high end commercial areas, and condos."

"They need these Creekside properties for the marina and the major shopping area," said Kyle pointing.

"Now we know why these people are aggressively purchasing property," said Lauren. "This has to be a multi-million dollar development."

"I would say 'billion,' said Kyle reaching for the rest of the papers on Lauren's lap. "And they really want the LaCrosse property."

Kyle handed Lauren the papers he was holding. It was a map of the LaCrosse property enlarged. In red someone had written 'key piece.' Attached to the map, was a color brochure full of renderings detailing a planned gated community.

"Oh my goodness," Lauren cried. "They want this whole island. There won't be anything left for us by the time they're finished."

"But Lauren, you already figured that out," Jefferson reminded her gently. "What's shown here shouldn't come as a surprise to you."

"I know," said Lauren. "It just hurts to see it all drawn out like that. Those people who have already sold their property will have nothing to come home to."

"Here's another map of another piece of property," said Kyle. "The brochure is showing a conservation subdivision."

"Where is that property?" asked Lauren.

"Comparing it to the big map, it's a piece of property on the south side of the island," said Kyle.

"Can you hand me that tax map, please?" Lauren asked pointing to the coffee table.

Kyle unfolded the document and handed it to his wife.

"Let's see who owns it," Lauren said looking for the property on the map. Finding it she read, "Simpson et al."

"Do you know them?" Kyle asked.

"Yeah, that's Walter Simpson," Jefferson said. "But I didn't know he still owned that property. In fact, I thought his daughter sold it after he died last year because I didn't think there were any black folks left on that side of the island."

"Neither did I," said Lauren. "Look, Oak Creek runs right through the property."

"That's the same creek on this brochure," said Kyle. "That's what makes it a conservation subdivision. The idea is to build homes without altering any of the natural habitats."

"Do we think we should tell people about all of this development that's coming?" asked Lauren.

"I don't know, Lauren," said Kyle. "What do you think folks on the island can do? If the Wessler-Forrest people own the land, they can put on it whatever the hell they want."

"But if they know what's going on with the land, maybe people won't sell."

"Ladies and gentlemen," said Jefferson. "I think we have found Delmar's killer."

"The Wessler-Forrest Corporation," Lauren concluded.

"I believe so. If Delmar stumbled onto this information, the corporation most likely didn't want him leaking this information and affecting their sales. Plus, on your grandmother and aunt's property, they've written 'key piece'. There's no telling what they would do to get their hands on that property, including killing the one person who could persuade them not to sell."

"And they're probably the same sick people who ran you off the road, Baby," said Kyle patting his wife's hand.

"Oh man," Lauren groaned. Suddenly, she felt sick. "It all fits...All of it."

"I will bet any amount of money that Kyle is right," said Jefferson. "And that makes me even more determined to go through all of the records listing white SUVs registered for this area and find the evidence to put these people away. Meanwhile, I'm bringing in the CEO for questioning."

"Before you do," said Lauren reaching for something on the coffee table. "Read this file. I guarantee it will strengthen your case."

Chapter 21

"Come on in, Netta," Lauren heard her mother say when she answered the door. "She's in the family room." Lauren quickly put away the development papers she was still reading and turned on the television.

The door to the family room opened and in walked Netta dressed sharply in a navy pants suit that accentuated her extremely slender and tall figure. Lauren figured she must have just come from showing a house. The two cousins stared awkwardly at one another for a moment before Netta broke the silence.

"I heard you got in an accident," she said. "I came to see how you're doing."

"I'm well, thanks for asking. I just hurt my knee," Lauren indicated her right leg that was propped up on the ottoman. "The doctor at the hospital told me to rest it for a day or two. Other than that, I'm fine."

"That's good," Netta said nervously.

"How's business?" Lauren asked politely but coolly.

"Growing actually. I had to get someone in to manage all of the paperwork," Netta responded.

"Really? Then Aunt Eleanor must really be out of the loop because she told me that you were struggling with the mainland properties."

Netta was slow in her response. "It's hard to sell mainland properties. People coming to these areas want to live on the islands, you know?"

Lauren thought about the brochures she was hiding. "Actually I do."

The two cousins grew silent. A couple of minutes went by before Netta broke the silence. "Look Lauren. I came to apologize for the other day at Duke's. You were trying to tell me about Delmar's death and I guess I just wanted it to be a simple robbery so I wouldn't have to think that someone did this to him on purpose. I'm sorry."

Lauren smiled for two reasons. First, Netta had never apologized to her before. Secondly, for the first time ever, they could resolve a situation on their own without Delmar mediating. Maybe there was hope for their friendship to survive without Delmar after all.

"I accept your apology," said Lauren.

Netta plopped down on the couch next to her. "Good. Now, how's your investigation coming along?"

"It's interesting," said Lauren. "I found out that a huge corporation is coming to develop Oak Grove Island."

"Really?" Netta responded casually. "What kind of development?"

"You name it," said Lauren. "Subdivisions, golf courses, high end commercial."

Lauren decided not to go into details about the plans that were made for the LaCrosse property. Remembering the conversation in the General Store parking lot, Lauren couldn't be entirely sure that Aunt Eleanor wasn't planning on selling her property. The very possibility chilled Lauren to the bone. She did ask Netta if she thought Aunt Eleanor had any plans for her acres.

"Who knows what that old bat is planning," Netta said bitterly. "That is the most stingy old woman I ever did come across. She never wanted to give me and my sisters anything. Like it was our fault that her son went to jail. He couldn't do wrong in her eyes. She worshipped the ground he walked on. Even after he did all that and he and Mama came home from the pen, she let them build a house on the land."

"I thought she let you and Derek build also," Lauren asked her.

"Yeah, but she wouldn't *sell* us a piece. She just kept it all in her name. She got 500 acres. What's a couple of acres out of 500?"

"What's wrong with her keeping it all in her name?" asked Lauren confused at Netta's anger. "Maybe it's her intention to pass down all of the acres when she passes on."

"Don't you see? With her keeping all of her acres in her name, she gets to control everything. She could sell it out from under us when she gets good and ready."

"Do you think she'd do that?" Lauren asked in alarm.

"I told you, there's no telling," Netta snapped bitterly.

"I still have yet to see your house," said Lauren, changing the subject before Netta completely boiled over and they were back at square one. "You finished it last year, right?"

"A little over a year ago," said Netta. "It's been great. Beats all of us living in that cramped apartment on the mainland. When I got pregnant with Troy, we had no idea where we would put him."

Lauren remembered all too well what her cousin had gone through. Netta and Derek had two children, Danice, who was six and Troy, who was a few months younger than Justin. Derek hadn't even been present for the first four years of Danice's life because he was serving time for drug possession. He had gotten out early on good behavior, but those years without her husband had been extremely hard for Netta. Without a college degree, her job choices were extremely limited. She finally got a job at a mainland supermarket that paid minimum wage but she had to move back home with Eleanor. Most of her money went to her grandmother for renting her old room. Plus she had to pay Eleanor to watch Danice, while she worked.

"I done raised my children and my grandchildren. I'll be damned if I'm going to raise my great-grandchildren too!" Eleanor had told her while holding out her hand for her weekly $30.

Under the same roof again, Netta and Eleanor were constantly at each other's throats. It was so bad that as soon as Derek was released from prison, the three of them found a one-bedroom apartment (that was all they could afford) on the mainland.

Meanwhile, Derek had found work as a mechanic in his uncle's garage and the young couple was finally able to afford a two bedroom apartment. Netta wasn't satisfied working for minimum wage with very little benefits so she went to night school to learn real estate. It took two years, but she finally got her license.

Lauren was happy that Netta finally founded something that she wanted to do. She knew that her cousin had traveled a hard road. Lauren also knew that Netta blamed her grandmother for a lot of her trouble. She couldn't really blame Netta for feeling that way because Eleanor barely gave her anything, not even love. When it came down to it, she and Delmar were the lucky ones. Lauren knew if she or Delmar had been faced with Netta's predicament, they would have been in much better shape living with Lazarus and Henrietta. Her Grandma was kind and loving to all of her grandchildren. Everything that she had, she would give to her children with no question. And she always knew what everyone needed.

Henrietta saw the hardness in her sister-in-law and extended love to Netta in the hope that it would counteract the resentfulness that she could see growing in her grand-niece. Netta's sisters long gave up seeking the approval of Eleanor, but for some reason, Netta kept holding on for something that her grandmother simply refused to give her. And as strange as it sounded, Eleanor probably resented Netta for that too.

"Well I should be going," said Netta rising from the chair.

"Okay," said Lauren. "I'm glad you stopped by."

"Are you headed back soon?" Netta asked.

"I'm here for a few more days."

"Good. Then I'll stop by again."

"That'll be nice."

Chapter 22

"Hey Lauren. John told me you were here for a while. It's good to see you in church this morning."

"Hi Aunt Philomena," Lauren responded as she took a program from one of the young Larson kids. "It's good to see you too."

"Where's Kyle?" Aunt Philomena inquired also taking a program. "Is he back in Macon?"

"No, actually he's parking the car," Lauren responded. "He should be in in a minute."

Kyle came in and greeted Aunt Philomena. Then they found a seat next to Marne. Lauren quietly admired her mother's coral linen dress and matching jacket.

"No, you can't borrow it," she teased. "The last thing your sister admired ended up in Florida."

Lauren laughed. "After service, maybe you can at least tell me where you bought it so I can get one like it?"

"I'll think about it. Now hush. Service is about to begin."

It was the third Sunday at Rock of Ages A.M.E. Church, a small church that had been on Oak Grove ever since the islanders settled there. The third Sunday meant that the Men's Choir would be singing, which was the reason John was in the choir stand and not sitting with them in their traditional right side, fourth row pew.

Pastor Lockhart gave a good sermon on maintaining faith in the midst of adversity. The message seemed to speak directly to Lauren. She didn't understand why her family was made to suffer such a loss. It was very difficult to have faith in knowing that there was a purpose for someone losing their life so soon, especially someone who was doing his best to protect others.

After Pastor Lockheart gave the Benediction, Lauren and Kyle tried to head for the door but they were swarmed by relatives who made up the majority of the congregation.

"Lauren," said Aunt Tessie, who'd come in after the announcements and had taken a seat behind them. "I heard you were in an accident. Are you okay?"

"I'm fine," Lauren responded. "I just banged up my leg. It's still a little sore."

"Yeah, I saw you limping in," said Aunt Tiny, John's youngest sister. Of course she was called that because she was in fact a tiny woman. At 4'8, she was shorter than Lauren but her big hair, which was now piled on top of her head, made up for her lack of height.

"You ought to have stayed home and off that leg," she fussed as she hugged Lauren and her nose was instantly filled with the sweet smell of her perfume. "Kyle, you couldn't get her to rest?"

"I tried, Aunt Tiny," Kyle responded. "But she really wanted to come to church this morning."

"There's nothing wrong with wantin' to come on out and worship the Lord," said Aunt Tessie. "Don't you listen to this little heathen."

"Who are you callin' a 'little heathen'?" Tiny fussed at her older sister. "I come to church more than you!"

Tessie and Tiny were always fussing at each other about something or another. Their arguments weren't taken very seriously, as it was always done in love. Lauren and Kyle exchanged looks. This could take a while. They needed to find a way to extricate themselves from this position as quickly as possible or else they would be forced to choose sides.

"Aunt Tessie and Aunt Tiny, we'll be seeing you. I see Netta over there and I want to say hello."

"Y'all speakin'?" asked Tiny, temporarily forgetting her argument with Tessie.

"Yeah, why wouldn't we be?" Asked Lauren confused.

Oak Grove was a small island but she had a hard time believing that her argument with Netta a few days ago had reached her aunts, unless Grandma told them. But she really didn't see her doing that.

"I didn't think you would be speakin' to her once you knew –"

Tessie nudged Tiny.

The gesture wasn't lost on Lauren, however.

"Knew what?" She asked looking from one aunt to the other.

"Y'all talkin' 'bout Netta Skinner?" asked Sarah Porter an old friend of the sisters, who had a thing for wearing dead animals around her neck, even in mid-80 degree weather. Today it was a fox, complete with head and paws.

"Hi Miss Sarah," Lauren greeted, unable to take her eyes off of the poor animal. She was creeped out by the glassy eyes staring at her. "Kyle, you remember Miss Sarah?"

Sarah Porter lived up the road from Lauren's parents.

"I sure do," said Kyle reaching for a hug in spite of the furry stole. "How're you doing Miss Sarah?"

"Ooh I'm fine, honey," Sarah said delighted to be remembered by Kyle. "Lauren, you snagged a good one honey."

Lauren laughed.

"You both got to stop by before y'all head back to Macon. How long you stayin'?"

"A few days," Lauren answered politely enough but she hoped she could get away from Oak Grove without making a trip to Miss Sarah's house. In addition to wearing dead things on her neck, she had dead things nailed to her wall. Then not forgetting why Miss Sarah came over in the first place, Lauren asked them about Netta.

"Girl, that chile sidin' with the enemy!" said Miss Sarah obviously relieved to let go of that secret. "She goin' 'round convincin' these families to sell their land!"

"*She's what*?!" Lauren exclaimed.

"Yes girl," said Tiny, succumbing to gossip, forgetting that church services ended ten minutes ago. "She's making a lot of money off the commission because those properties are selling for several million dollars."

"I don't believe it!" Lauren cried out. "I thought she was selling homes on the mainland."

"She was, but ain't nobody tryin' to buy no house on the mainland. These islands is where the real money at. The island land is the prime real estate. She sell that and she making money. Then when they build on it, she can turn around and sell that too."

Then Lauren remembered the other day when Netta told her that she wasn't moving properties on the mainland.

"Please, them white folks ain't gonna let Netta sell them developments," Tessie spoke up. "They just usin' her to get folks' property."

"Well now I know why she said she needed an assistant! How could she do this?" Lauren asked feeling betrayed. "We're struggling to keep our land and she's handing it over to developers on a silver platter!"

"Hmph! She don't care nothin' 'bout that," said Miss Sarah crossing her arms.

"I've got to get out of here," Lauren gathered her purse and headed for the exit.

Kyle was on her heels. She managed to get a few friendly words out to Pastor Lockhart, who was meeting all of the parishioners at the door, before leaving.

Netta spying her cousin walking out the door caught up with her.

"Hey Lauren," she said brightly.

Lauren stopped short and looked at her cousin as if she was seeing her for the first time.

"Don't 'hey' me, you sellout!" Lauren spat her words at her with as much fierceness as she could muster.

Netta's smile melted from her face. "Who told you?"

"Doesn't matter," Lauren spoke. "The point is that you broke a promise that we made to Lazarus!"

"I did not!" Netta replied angrily. "I didn't sell LaCrosse property!"

"Just everyone else's land right? So that makes it okay?"

"Let me tell you something, Lauren," Netta said wagging a finger in her face. "If I don't sell those properties, somebody else will. You either step on or get stepped on. I got a family to feed and children to clothe, and if you can't understand that, then that is too damn bad!"

"What happened to you?" Lauren asked not believing what she was hearing.

"I just grew up, Lauren. Life ain't no sunshine and roses and we ain't gonna have nothin' unless we take it!"

Lauren looked away from her to see several parishioners trying to act as if they weren't listening to their argument.

When she looked back at her cousin, she said ever so softly, "Now I see why you got so upset when I said Delmar died because of the land. Your little slippery self is mixed all up and through this entire mess. As far as I'm concerned, you're just as guilty for Delmar's death as the one who actually pulled the trigger."

With those words spoken, Lauren stormed away from her cousin. She was done with Netta. Done. There would be no more, "Tell her I saids," and not because Delmar was dead. There would be no more because Lauren refused to say anything else to Netta for a very long while.

Chapter 23

After church, the family had Sunday dinner at Grandma Henrietta's. For obvious reasons, Netta did not come to the house. Lauren, who usually looked forward to island home-cooking, was too angry to eat. Instead of eating after the blessing, she passed through the dining room where all of the relatives were hungrily making their way through the buffet. Lauren pulled open the sliding glass door and stepped out onto the screen porch, the intense sea air instantly filling her nose. She could hear the wind whipping across the high sand dunes a few yards away. It was easy to see why a developer would be salivating to seize this piece of land.

Frustrated, Lauren plopped down on the wicker love seat which had long since replaced the cots the cousins used as their beds during their many sleepovers, and kicked off her high heeled sandals. Lauren closed her eyes and listened as the waves crashed against the shore. Lauren didn't hear the door slide open and did not notice that someone had entered the porch until she heard, "How are you, Lauren?"

Lauren's eyes snapped open with surprise. "Mom! I didn't hear you come in."

"I know you didn't," said Marne chuckling as she sat down in the love seat next to her. "You looked like you were in another world."

"Sometimes, I wish I were in another world," Lauren sighed.

"You've been having a hard time of it lately, haven't you?" Said Marne with a sympathetic look in her brown eyes.

Lauren had those same eyes. As she looked at her mother sitting next to her, she realized that she could see Justin in her eyes as well. Just as Justin's features were compared to Lauren's, Lauren's features were compared to Marne's. Everywhere Lauren went, people said that she and Marne looked just alike. They had the same button nose and thick hair. Until recently, Marne had always worn her hair short. Now it was longer and flat ironed, furthering the resemblance between mother and daughter.

Right at that moment, as Lauren took comfort in her mother with her head on her shoulder, she felt like a little girl again. She didn't want her resemblance to Marne to end with just the physical. Lauren hoped that she'd also inherited her mother's nurturing spirit that she could pass that along to her son when he needed it. It was that spirit

Marne was using to comfort her daughter as the two sat in one of the most memorable spots of Lauren's childhood.

"So, what were you and Netta arguing about in church?" asked Marne breaking the silence.

"Oh you heard about that, huh?" said Lauren a little embarrassed that their disagreement had reached her mother.

"Yes. I figured it was pretty bad if you were arguing two minutes after services ended."

"Yeah, I'm sorry about that," Lauren apologized lifting her head from Marne's shoulder.

"So? Are you going to spill it or what?" Marne asked after Lauren did not elaborate.

"Mom, I found out that Netta is the real estate agent who's selling off people's properties!" Lauren finally let it all out as if a dam had broken.

"Yes, your father and I were hoping that you wouldn't find out about that," said Marne a bit sheepishly.

"*You knew?!*" Lauren exclaimed. "Mom, why didn't you guys tell me?"

She felt betrayed that her parents withheld such important information.

"Because your father and I didn't want this to affect your friendship with Netta."

"It doesn't really take much to do that," Lauren grumbled.

"I know that you and Netta are prone to argue. That has been pretty much the nature of your relationship. But you feel so strongly about the land remaining in the hands of the islanders to the point that we thought that you finding out about Netta's involvement could *destroy* your relationship. We just didn't want to see that happen."

"You were definitely right to think that. I can't tolerate sellouts and liars," Lauren said judgmentally.

"What did Netta lie about?" Marne asked confused.

"That girl looked my grandfather in the eye and swore to him that she would never sell the LaCrosse land."

"And she hasn't sold it," Marne pointed out.

"Well it's only a matter of time before she does. With her acting as the agent for all of the other properties, you think those developers are going to let her stop short of this land?" asked Lauren indicating the beach in the distance.

"Lauren, you don't know that at all," protested Marne.

"I don't know what I know," said Lauren frustrated.

"Lauren, I know how you feel. Believe me I do. Your Grandpa Lawrence told me the same thing about the developers buying up all of the land and destroying our way of life when I was growing up down south. Now our family didn't sell our land, but everyone else sold theirs. The point is that our family still owns property on the island that is now considered to be built-out with expensive development. The other families that sold out now have nothing to go back to and they have nothing to leave their descendants. In the end Sweetheart, it's the choice of the individual, and sometimes it's a bad one. You can't put all the blame on Netta."

"Mom, I know you're trying to help," said Lauren. "But I blame Netta because she knows better. She knows that we as a people are fighting to hold onto what's ours and she goes out and sides with the enemy."

"So you just want to be upset for a while?" Marne asked understanding her daughter's stubborn mood.

"I don't *want* to be upset, I just am. I just feel like we're never going to have anything because there will always be someone who puts the almighty dollar before building a legacy. Don't you see? We're always sabotaging our own people. It's like what Daddy always said: Those slave traders would have never gotten the Africans if their own people didn't show them where to go to get them. And in the end, the sellouts were chained on the boat with the rest of them, looking like 'Boo Boo the Fool'."

Marne laughed with her daughter, who managed to laugh also, in spite of herself. She gave Lauren a big hug.

"I promise that one day you're going to feel better about everything," she said. "And it'll never be okay that Delmar's dead, but in time, the pain will subside. I promise."

"Thanks Mom," said Lauren hugging her mother back.

"So are you ready to come back in and get something to eat?" Marne asked after they let go.

"In a minute," said Lauren wanting to enjoy the tranquility a little more.

"Make it quick, because Aunt Vicki's got your husband cornered."

"Oh no," said Lauren quickly rising from the love seat. "Mom, why didn't you tell me that sooner?"

Aunt Vicki was married to Uncle Luke, John's youngest brother. She had a tendency to go on and on with the most boring stories known to man. What made it worse is that she had a huge gap in her teeth and causing her to spit when she talked.

One Thanksgiving dinner when Lauren was about thirteen, she told Lauren an hour-long story about a wart that had formed on her left index finger. If she hadn't finally interrupted and told Aunt Vicki that her mother was probably looking for her, Lauren would still be talking to her this very moment.

"I knew that would get you moving," Marne said following Lauren into the dining room, where sure enough her husband was in a chair next to Aunt Vicki who was talking his ear off.

Kyle shot Lauren a "help me" look while trying to discreetly wipe away the spittle that kept sprinkling his face.

Before she could get over there, Aunt Tiny exclaimed, "Girl, you sure got that Netta told!"

Everyone, including Aunt Vicki (to Kyle's relief) dropped what they were doing and took notice.

"Tiny, even though Netta acted a straight up fool, she's still family!" Aunt Philomena scolded as she helped herself to a slice of chocolate cake.

"What?" Tiny asked innocently. "Look, if your family can't call you out on your foolishness, then who can?"

Philomena knew that her sometimes abrasive sister had a point. So instead of trying to come up with a good enough comeback, she just shrugged her shoulders and went back to eating her cake.

Chapter 24

"Go on in and have a seat," Jefferson held open the door to the interrogation room for Bryce Wessler and his lawyer, Dan Dansbury.

"You hauled in Bryce Wessler? Are you crazy, Pierce?" Clyde looked up from his desk and scoffed. "Chief's gonna cut off your family jewels and hand them to you."

"Whatever man," Jefferson spat back. "Just make sure we're not disturbed. "

"It's your funeral," said Clyde returning to his reports.

Jefferson went into the interrogation room and firmly shut the door behind him.

"Perhaps you can tell us why you dragged my client in here," Dansbury said impatiently.

"I am investigating your client for the murder of Delmar LaCrosse."

"You can't be serious!" Wessler exclaimed. "Based on what?"

"We'll sue this station for false arrest!" Dansbury bellowed.

"Mr. Wessler, you are connected to the last project that Mr. LaCrosse was working on," Jefferson answered. "And you are not under arrest yet. I just need you to answer a few questions."

"What kind of questions?" Dansbury demanded to know.

"It's okay, Dan," Bryce told his lawyer. "Detective Pierce thinks dragging me in here makes him feel like he's doing something towards solving this case. I'll play along and answer his questions."

"Are you sure?"

"It's fine. I've got nothing to hide."

"How did you know Mr. LaCrosse?" Jefferson asked with his pen poised over the legal pad he'd brought in for note-taking.

"We met occasionally at the town council meetings."

"And you had business with the council?"

"Obviously."

"What kind of business?"

"I had a few rezonings that I needed approved."

"When you say 'a few,' how many is that exactly – ?"

"Really!" interrupted Mr. Dansbury impatiently. "Is that relevant?"

"Yes. So how many rezonings, Mr. Wessler?" Jefferson repeated the question.

"Fifteen," answered Bryce Wessler.

"Fifteen?"

"Yes. One five. Fifteen."

Jefferson wrote it down and asked, "So how many of the fifteen did Mr. LaCrosse recommend for approval?"

"Approximately six."

"Did he give a reason for the ones he disapproved?"

"Does it make a difference?" Wessler asked.

"Yes."

"Do I have to answer?" Wessler asked his attorney.

"No you most certainly do not," Dansbury stated firmly.

"That's okay," said Jefferson and he tossed a file on the table in front of Wessler.

"What's this?" asked Wessler opening the file.

"They are articles from the Oak Grove Gazette written about the rezonings," Jefferson answered smugly. "According to the articles, the reason Mr. LaCrosse did not approve the majority of the rezonings is that it didn't fit into the land uses outlined for the future."

"So? What are you trying to say?"

"I'm just saying that I'm confused as to why you wanted to hide that fact, especially since the council passed the rezonings anyway. Except for the last one Delmar brought before council."

"What's your point?" Mr. Dansbury asked.

"I'm just wondering why all these rezonings had been passed in spite of being recommended for disapproval by Mr. LaCrosse, but this last one, a residential subdivision that calls for four homes to the acre, was not approved."

"How would I know that?" Bryce shifted uncomfortably in his seat.

"Well according to this article, the survey of how much of these 200 acres you actually owned was in question."

"Okay," Mr. Dansbury spoke up suddenly. "I'm putting an end to this. If you're not charging my client, we're out of here. Let's go Bryce."

But Jefferson wasn't finished.

"So if Mr. LaCrosse was the one to uncover this information about this piece of property – property you wanted – maybe he was too threatening for you to have around. And it was Mr. LaCrosse who uncovered these questions, according to the news articles. So it could be argued that you had a reason to harm Mr. LaCrosse."

"Let's go," said Dansbury rising.

"One more question," said Jefferson. "Where were you on the night of May 15th, between the hours of 9 and 11 pm?

"At a party for one of my investors, P.T. Hollingsworth," Wessler responded importantly. "You can call and check it out. At least 50 people can account for the fact that I was there."

"I will most certainly check it out," said Jefferson meeting Bryce Wessler's cold blue eyes. "You gentlemen have a good day."

Without another word, the lawyer and his client walked out of the interrogation room, letting the door slam behind them.

Jefferson went to his desk and picked up the phone.

"Lauren," he said when she answered. "Those newspaper articles you found on the rezonings hit the jackpot. Wessler was so nervous that he was shaking in his chair."

When Jefferson had come up empty with the council minutes, it had suddenly occurred to Lauren that the council meetings were likely to be covered in the local newspaper. She had gotten to work immediately and copied the periodicals from the library. Upon carefully reviewing the articles, Lauren could barely contain herself the morning she ran across the information about the rezonings.

"So, do you think he did it?" Lauren asked barely daring to breath. "Do you think that greedy monster murdered my cousin?"

"Yes, Lauren. I do."

Chapter 25

"Morning Daddy," said Lauren coming into the kitchen the next morning.

John looked up from the paper he was reading at the kitchen table.

"Morning Lauren. How's your leg doing this morning?"

"It's getting better," said Lauren going over to the counter for a muffin. After pouring herself a glass of orange juice, she joined her father at the kitchen table and began to eat.

"Lauren."

Lauren looked up from her light breakfast to find her father staring at her intently. "Are you being careful?" he asked.

"What do you mean?" Lauren asked but she had a good idea what her father meant. She was stalling for time because she didn't want to answer.

"Lauren, you didn't just run off the road did you?" John asked straight out.

Lauren looked at her father who was staring at her intently

"No Daddy."

"Lauren, you're a grown woman and I don't want to tell you what to do..." John let out a trouble sigh. "I really wish you and Kyle would go back to Macon."

"Daddy, I have to find – "

"I know," he interrupted. "You have to find Delmar's killer. Lauren, that huge development that you uncovered is a big deal. The fact they kept it hidden means there are some very heavy hitters that are involved. These people could have very well killed Delmar and they are very good with covering their tracks. You might have to let this go, Sweetheart."

Lauren put down the muffin that she was eating. She suddenly lost her appetite.

"Daddy, do you know how close Delmar and I were?"

"You're my daughter. I've watched you your whole life. Of course I know how close you two were."

"I don't think you do," said Lauren looking at her fingers, "We were blood cousins."

"Lauren, you're first cousins. What else would you be?"

"No, you don't understand," said Lauren chuckling softly. "You know that old oak on Grandma's land down by the creek? The one with the limbs that are close to the ground and seem to stretch on forever?"

"Yeah, I know that tree," said John. "Tom and I used to play out there. I guess it's only fitting that our children would love that tree also."

"It was our hideout. Delmar and I would go out there to play and plan our future."

"Where was Netta?"

"Under Aunt Eleanor's thumb most likely. After Uncle Micah died, she couldn't play with us anymore" Lauren let out a sad sigh at the memory. "That day was one of the days we had to go to Grandma and Granddad's after school because you guys had to go to the mainland for something or other. The kids were making fun of my new glasses. I was so upset that I ran straight off the bus and kept running until I found myself at the tree. Delmar followed me out there to cheer me up. He told me that the kids were jealous because the glasses made me look smart or something like that. I told him that I knew I looked corny and he should be laughing at me also. Delmar told me that he would never laugh at me because we're not only family, but we were best friends. Then he got this idea to be blood cousins."

"What's blood cousins?" John asked smiling.

"Well Delmar took this pocket knife, you know the one Granddad gave to him and he pricked his finger with it. It bled a lot too. I was scared but I let him prick my finger too. Then we pressed them together. Then we promised to always be close and not to let anyone hurt us"

"That's really special."

"It was disgusting, actually with all of that blood!" Lauren laughed at the memory. "There's still a spot on the tree from it. But you're right, Dad. It was special too. And that's why I can't let people just call Delmar's murder a robbery. He was so much better than that. He deserves justice and I'm the only one who can get it for him."

Chapter 26

Lauren stared at her copies of the rezoning articles thinking that Bryce Wessler benefited the most with Delmar out of the way. All they needed now was the proof that linked the powerful developer to the murder. That was easier said than done.

Lauren tossed the articles onto the ottoman and ran her fingers through her thick hair. Kyle chose that moment to walk into the family room. He took in his wife's disheveled appearance and tried not to let her see the worry on his face. He knew that Lauren was obsessed with this case. She hadn't been eating properly and she was dreaming about something every night. Lauren was already a wild sleeper during the best of times, but her foot kept finding his shins more often than usual as she fought off invisible demons in the middle of the night.

"Wow that's a new look," said Kyle trying to mask his concern with some light teasing.

Lauren took her fingers out of her hair. "Yeah, I thought I would try something different." Her eyes fell on the cordless phone sitting on the coffee table.

"He'll call, Lauren," Kyle assured her.

"I know. I'm just anxious to see if he found out anything else."

The doorbell rang just then and Lauren sprung quickly to her feet.

"I'll get it," said Kyle easing her back into the chair.

"I'm perfectly capable of getting the door," Lauren fussed at him.

"I know you are but I'm already up," Kyle answered and left the room. He came back into the family room with Jefferson.

"Hey Jefferson," said Lauren. "What's the word?"

Jefferson took a seat on the couch.

"First," Jefferson began. "The Rashads were arraigned at 10 o'clock this morning. Bail was set at one million dollars."

"One million dollars?!" Lauren exclaimed. "They don't have that kind of money!"

"Exactly."

"What are they going to do about raising bail?" asked Kyle concerned.

"Sell something I guess or remain in jail."

"This crazy," Lauren shook her head. "Do I even want to know the rest of what you have to tell us?"

"I think Wessler is hiding something about the property that was denied rezoning. Call it a hunch, but he was way too nervous when I questioned him. Whatever it was, I think Delmar may have found out about it, giving Wessler a motive for murder."

"We need to find out what it is," Lauren said impatiently. "I don't have any more patience for speculation. We need hard evidence!"

"Lauren, I'm going out tonight to the property and look around," Jefferson told her.

"Great. I'm going with you," Lauren decided.

"The hell you are!" Jefferson protested. "It is way too dangerous."

"Try and stop me," Lauren said stubbornly.

"Lauren," said Kyle firmly. "They've already tried to run you off the road. I don't even want to think about what else they would do if they found out you were out there snooping around."

"I have to go, Kyle. I might see something out there that Jefferson would miss."

"Lauren. I'm a detective," Jefferson reminded her.

"And I'm a planner," said Lauren. "I know what would spook a developer. Do you?"

"I can't let you go out there, Lauren," said Kyle losing his patience. "Your father would have my head!"

"Mine too!" Jefferson concurred.

"Who says he has to know?" Lauren challenged.

"Lauren, it is too dangerous," Kyle insisted.

"Kyle, I'm sorry but I'm going."

Kyle took a deep breath and rubbed his goatee. He knew he was not going to win this one. "Then I'm going with you. Besides, I'm a planner too if we're using your logic. In fact, you should stay here while I go."

Lauren shook her head furiously.

"Guys," said Jefferson holding his hands up. I cannot let you take this risk."

"I'm going." Lauren folded her arms, which meant that was the end of the discussion.

"And if Lauren is going, then I'm going," Kyle said just as firmly.

"Fine, since I can't talk either of you out of it, meet me on the north side of the property on Coral Road at 7:30. The sun will start to go down by then and we can sneak on without being seen."

"Glad that's settled," said Lauren.

"And now for the next order of business," Jefferson pulled out a thick folder. "Here is a list of all of the late model white Ford Explorers in the county. There are almost 300 of them."

"*Three hundred*?!" Lauren exclaimed as she took the file Jefferson handed her.

Kyle just shook his head.

"I managed to go through and highlight the ones registered in Oak Grove. The good news is that there are only four of those."

"Toby Armstrong, Keith Sampson, Alaina White, and Smiley Jones," Kyle read through the highlighted names. Anybody sound familiar?"

"Well a couple of names sound familiar. We know all of the native families on the island. I'm not familiar with 'Sampson,' though."

"Okay," said Jefferson writing down the name in a small pad. "He'll have to be checked out."

He put the pen back in his pocket and looked at Lauren and Kyle.

"I can't do anything else official after this point," he said. "In fact, I'm taking a great risk going out to that south side property."

"Why is that?" Lauren asked fearing the answer.

"Well the chief had a real problem with me bringing in Bryce Wessler for questioning. In fact, the Big Wig Councilman Whitman made a huge stink out of it."

"I just bet he did," Lauren grumbled.

"What did they do, Jefferson?" Kyle asked catching on a bit quicker than his wife.

"They suspended me from the police force.

Chapter 27

"I cannot believe those fools suspended him," Lauren said for what must have been the tenth time since Jefferson delivered the news.

"He was getting too close," Kyle responded, lightly tapping the steering wheel.

The two were sitting in their minivan on Coral Road waiting for Jefferson to arrive.

"What time is it?" Lauren had asked that same question about ten times also.

"It's two minutes since the last time you asked," said Kyle looking at the dashboard clock.

"It's a quarter to eight," Lauren said as if she didn't hear Kyle. "What's keeping him?"

"He'll be here soon, Lor," said Kyle patiently.

"What if he's already here?" Lauren asked.

"His car isn't here," Kyle said logically.

Lauren looked around and realized he was right. She looked to the west to see the sun sinking behind the trees.

"The sun will be totally down soon and we won't be able to see anything. If he's not here in five minutes, we're going in without him."

"Lauren, be reasonable," Kyle groaned. His wife, although usually agreeable, could be at times a very determined woman, but now she was teetering on obsessive.

"Kyle," Lauren said firmly. "If he's not here in five minutes, I'm going in without him."

"Okay," Kyle found himself surrendering again. "We'll give Jefferson five more minutes."

The moments ticked by slowly, but not slowly enough for Kyle. Going in with Jefferson was one thing. At least he was a trained officer and could provide them with protection. But to go into this dense area at night was dangerous, particularly with a killer on the loose. Kyle didn't doubt that he could protect his wife if he had to, but he didn't feel good about exposing her to this situation in the first place. He found himself desperately hoping that Jefferson would show up in the next three minutes. At one point a pair of headlights shined on the couple, but they were immediately in the dark again as the car passed them.

"Kyle," Lauren's voice cut through the silence. "It's 8 minutes to 8 o'clock."

Sighing inwardly, Kyle grabbed the two flashlights from the glove compartment and reached for the door.

"Come on. Let's go."

"Wait Kyle," Lauren stopped him from getting out of the car. "I don't think we have to go on foot yet. There's a little road up ahead we can use to access the property."

Relieved, Kyle closed his door.

"How are we going to go through 200 acres at night anyway," Kyle asked as a last ditch effort to make his wife see reason.

He put the car in gear and headed for the access road.

"I don't expect to go through all 200 acres," Lauren responded. "What we need to do is start with the piece of property that Wessler thought he owned."

"What do expect to find there?" Asked Kyle as he navigated the dark road.

"Don't know, but we have to start somewhere," said Lauren. "Pull in here for a moment, please."

Kyle did as he was instructed and they found themselves in someone's yard. A few feet away was a dark, small, worn out house. The wood had rotted making the roof cave in and the large front porch sag. All of the windows were either broken or missing.

"That's the Simpson home," Lauren said softly. "I don't think anyone has lived in it since he died."

"Do you know the daughter?"

"No, not really. I just heard that he had one. She's like Dad's age." Lauren opened the door and hopped out of the car.

"Maybe you can ask him about her," said Kyle following suit.

"Maybe. I hope we don't run into any wild animals," said Lauren shining her light in front of her. Though they were in a clearing, it was surrounded by dense wood.

"I can think of worse things to run into," Kyle said wryly. After a few moments of watching Lauren swinging her light in every direction, he asked, "What are we looking for?"

"We're looking for something that would attract a developer,"

"All I see are trees."

Lauren sighed as she realized her husband was right. "Yeah, me too."

She headed back to the car with Kyle following. He opened her door for her and the dome light lit the interior. Lauren caught a glimpse of the rendered brochure of the conservation subdivision proposed for the property they were standing on.

"Hey, how come we didn't notice this before?" Lauren peered closer at the document.

"Notice what?" Kyle asked looking over her shoulder.

Why is lot 17 circled in red?" Lauren asked.

"Maybe there's something special about it," said Kyle. "Look how it sits right on the creek."

"Well so are five other lots," Lauren pointed out. "Maybe Wessler picked this lot out for himself?"

"Maybe," said Kyle tentatively.

"Can you tell where it is on the tax map?" Asked Lauren pulling it from beneath all of the other documents.

141

"About here," said Kyle pointing to a place on the map. "Where there's the big bend in the creek."

"I want to check it out," said Lauren.

"Lauren, it's dark out there," Kyle protested. "What do you expect to see?"

"I won't know until I see it."

"Why don't we come out here first thing in the morning? We'll have light then."

"Kyle, we're already here," Lauren said impatiently. "Besides, how do you know it will still be there in the morning?"

"How do we know *what* will still be there?" Kyle asked just as impatiently.

"I don't know, but I want to go now, Kyle."

Kyle sighed for what must have been the millionth time that evening. "Okay, but after we check it out, can we please save the rest of the sleuthing for the morning?"

"Yes," Lauren promised. "We can go home after. Thanks for doing this."

"I would do anything for you, you know that."

The couple was quiet as they rode along the road that led to the creek. When the moonlight broke through the trees, its light reflecting off of the clear water, Kyle stopped the car and the two got out again.

"Well there's the creek," said Kyle breaking the silence.

"Let's look around a bit," said Lauren refusing to give up just yet.

Kyle walked through a small thicket by the creek.

"Be careful in the tall grass!" Lauren called out to Kyle. "You don't know what's in there."

No sooner than the words were out of her mouth, Kyle tripped over something and fell to the ground.

"Kyle!" Lauren screamed and ran to him.

"Well," said Kyle sitting up to see what tripped him. "I know for a fact that *this* would have still been here in the morning or someone would have some serious explaining to do."

Lauren saw immediately what Kyle was talking about. "I don't believe it! I just don't believe it!"

"At least now we know what that fool was hiding: The final resting place of Haywood Simpson is sitting right on proposed lot 17," Kyle said dryly. "Born 1871, died 1931."

"Look, there are more headstones," said Lauren looking around. "Here's one dated 1883 and another one for 1901."

"So this is what Delmar found," said Kyle. "This is some big stuff. Do you realize what this means?"

Lauren didn't answer. Instead, she was standing very still and staring at something else in the tall grass.

"Lauren? Lauren, what's wrong?"

Lauren's answer came in a high pitched scream.

Chapter 28

Kyle scrambled to his feet and was immediately at Lauren's side.
"What's wrong? What did you scream for?" Kyle pulled at Lauren's hands that were clasping tightly against her mouth. She'd stop screaming but her eyes, wide with terror were still fixed on something.

Kyle followed her gaze to a grassy area that was visible in the moonlight. He took his flashlight and shined it on the spot anyway. He saw instantly what made Lauren scream. It was a foot. Kyle moved the beam up and saw the rest of the body sprawled face down in the dirt underneath a headstone that was so old and weathered, it was unreadable.

Kyle carefully made his way to the body and shined his light on the face.

"Oh my lord," he groaned. "It's Jefferson."

Chapter 29

"Lauren? Are you guys alright?" Marne ran up to her daughter with John closely in tow.

Kyle and Lauren were in the waiting room at the mainland hospital after having driven behind the ambulance that was carrying Jefferson.

"We're fine, Mom," Lauren replied holding her mother tightly.

"How's Jefferson?" John asked.

"It's bad," cried Lauren. "Really bad."

That's all she could get out before burying her head into her mother's chest. Marne patted her back soothingly.

"He was shot in the back," Kyle explained. "The bullet missed his heart but nicked an artery or something.

He's lost a lot of blood. The paramedics said if we hadn't found him when we did, he'd be dead right now."

"And that's still a possibility," said Lauren lifting up her head. "They lost the pulse a couple of times before he went up to the operating room."

John shook his head with disbelief. "Where did you find him?" he asked.

Lauren and Kyle anticipated this question and they decided to stick to as close to the truth as possible, omitting the details that would cause worry.

"Out by the Simpson property," said Kyle, telling them the same story that he told Mr. and Mrs. Pierce an hour earlier. "We were driving around and happened to find him."

"It's a good thing that you did," Marne commented. "Are his parents here yet?"

"Yes," said Lauren. "They arrived shortly after we did. Right now they're speaking to the surgeon."

"Who would do this to him?" Marne asked sadly.

"I don't know," said John taking her hand.

But Lauren and Kyle knew.

Lauren, Kyle, John, and Marne remained in the waiting room for most of the evening. Lauren flipped though magazines, not really reading them. Kyle and John were involved in a deep conversation, talking in low tones. Marne stared at the television, which was turned to CNN. More American troops were being deployed to Iraq.

Fifteen more minutes past before Mr. and Mrs. Pierce came into the waiting room. Both had expressions of intense pain etched into their faces. They walked in hand and hand over to where the LaCrosses were sitting. Lauren tossed her magazine aside and jumped up. The rest of the family followed suit.

"How is he?" Lauren asked anxiously.

"They still workin' on him," said Mr. Pierce evenly.

"Did they say how long the operation would be?"

"No tellin'. The bullet tore up a lot on the inside. God was looking out for him 'cause it missed his heart."

"Spencer and Anna, why don't you have a seat," John offered and Marne took Mrs. Pierce's arms to guide her to one of the cushioned seats.

"I meant to thank you two earlier for finding our boy," Mrs. Pierce told Lauren and Kyle.

"We're really sorry this happened to him," said Kyle.

"That's the risk of the job," said Mr. Pierce. "We were so proud when he made detective, but we were worried too. We tried not to show it 'cause Jefferson loved what he was doin'."

"He's very good at his job," said Lauren. "In fact –"

She caught the slight shake of Kyle's head. Lauren was well aware that she almost slipped up. Like they didn't want to worry Lauren's parents, it was probably best for the time being to divulge as little as possible as to the reason Jefferson was lying in the hospital.

But Mrs. Pierce prompted. "What child?"

"Um…uh…Just that Jefferson had been a big help to me when I got here," Lauren managed to finish.

"We were really sorry to hear about Delmar." Mrs. Pierce reached over and patted Lauren's hand. "I don't know when this island got to be so violent. We used to be peaceful people. Everybody knew everybody but now things are changin'. Useta be that we didn't hafta lock our doors, but now these people are comin' and takin' over, bringin' their devilish ways with them! Ain't no mo' peace now!"

Mr. Pierce put his arm around Mrs. Pierce and held her close.

The chief of police, accompanied by a couple of officers arrived to express support to the Pierces.

"We promise to find whoever did this to him," the chief promised. To Kyle and Lauren he said, "I understand that you're the ones who found Detective Pierce."

Kyle glanced at Lauren before he answered, "Yes, we did."

"I need to get your statement."

"Chief, I understand what you need, but my wife is distraught," said Kyle as he now glanced at the Pierces sitting huddled close together. He did not want to upset the couple with the details. "Can we possibly make our statement in the morning?"

"First thing in the morning," the chief confirmed. "We would like your statement while it's still fresh on your mind."

"Chief," Lauren whispered. "I promise I won't forget a single detail."

Chapter 30

It was one o'clock in the morning and Kyle and Lauren were still in the waiting room at the hospital. John and Marne had left a couple of hours ago after assuring the Pierces that everything would work out for the best. They promised to keep Jefferson in their prayers and asked the kids that they give an update when he was out of surgery.

The surgery had taken a lot longer than anticipated. The surgeon had come out to the waiting room about an hour ago to tell the Pierces that Jefferson had suffered more bleeding than they'd originally thought. It would take time to access and repair all of the internal damage. The events of the day had proven to be too much for Lauren and she'd fallen asleep with her head in Kyle's lap.

In her subconscious, Lauren became aware of the sudden change in the mood of the waiting room and she woke suddenly. The first thing she noticed were the Pierces sobbing intensely.

"What's going on?" Lauren asked cautiously. "Is Jefferson out of surgery? He's not…"

"He's out of surgery," said Kyle softly. "He's not dead, but he's in a coma."

"Oh no!"

"They've got him in the intensive care unit."

The Pierces gathered their belongings and headed down the hall.

"Where are they going?" asked Lauren.

"They're going to see Jefferson in the ICU," said Kyle. "I don't think there is too much more we can do here tonight, Lor."

"Okay," Lauren said sadly. She watched the retreating backs of Jefferson's parents as they walked down the hall.

"We'll come back tomorrow," said Kyle.

"Okay."

Before the couple gathered their belongings, a small woman wearing a turquoise warm-up suit and Ugg boots, came into the waiting room. Though it was after one in the morning, her makeup had been carefully applied to her strong features and her hair was combed into a neat French roll.

"Lauren, is that you?" The woman asked.

"Yes it is. Do I know you?" Lauren asked quizzically. The woman looked familiar but Lauren had a hard time placing her.

"I remember you from school. You were a couple of grades ahead of me. I'm Marva."

"Oh!" Lauren exclaimed finally realizing why she looked familiar. "You're Jefferson's cousin!"

Lauren reached out to hug her. "How are you holding up?"

"Not well at all," Marva replied. When she let go of Lauren, she noticed Kyle standing there.

"Oh, I'm sorry," Lauren realized. "Marva, this is my husband, Kyle."

"I'm so sorry about Jefferson," said Kyle also giving her a hug.

"Thank you. Do you know what's going on with him?"

Kyle gave her the details of his condition.

"Oh man," she said plopping down into a cushioned chair. "This is all my fault!"

"Your fault?" Lauren asked confused. "How could it be your fault? You're not the one who shot him."

"No, but I sent him running out there!"

"Marva, why don't you tell us what happened?" Kyle said to her.

"Okay," Marva sighed. "I know that Jefferson was trying to find out what really happened to Delmar – I am so sorry about that, by the way."

"Thank you," said Lauren.

"I don't know if Jeff told you that I'm Telly Whitman's assistant, you know the councilman?"

"Yes, he did."

"I hate working for him 'cause he's so slippery. That's why I'm going to community college on the mainland and get my degree working on computers so I can be up out of there. Anyway, Whitman's got it in his head that he's gonna become the mayor of Oak Grove at the next election, so he's bringin' in all of this development. If you ask me, I think it's so he can have the votes when they hold the election in two years, if you know what I mean, 'cause right now, ain't nobody tryin' to vote him into office. Too many black folks here. With all these hotels, condos, and stuff, he'll have enough of his kinda folks to vote him in 'cause once they get our land, there ain't gonna be no more black people for him to worry 'bout. Then too, you know how white folks think that anybody who bring in development should be the boss of everythin'. So basically, he killin' two birds with one stone."

Lauren and Kyle exchanged looks. Marva was onto something. Having her in Councilman Whitman's office had proven to be valuable. At least they now understood his underlying motivation for bringing in rapid development.

"So what happened tonight, Marva?" Lauren asked gently.

Marva shook her head. With a shaky voice, she continued. "I overheard a conversation Whitman was having with this guy, P.T. Hollingsworth in his office. I don't know why they brought their business in there 'cause the walls are thin and I can hear everything. Then again, maybe they think I'm too stupid to understand what they're up to. Anyway, they were talking about some property on the south side of the island that didn't get rezoned or something. I think it got turned down at the council meetin'. Whitman told Hollingsworth that he tried to get it through but legally, there was nothing they could do until they figured out who owned what. Then Hollingsworth asked when the rezoning would be appealed and Whitman told him it was canceled. Child, that's when the grits hit the fan, 'cause ole Hollingsworth lost it! He demanded that this guy somebody by the name of Brock Wesley –"

"Bryce Wessler?" Lauren asked.

"Yeah, that's it. I knew it was something like that – Bryce Wessler. Well Hollingsworth said that he'd better get it back before council. Then they said now that the nosy building inspector was taken care of – sorry Lauren – there shouldn't be no problems. Then Whitman said that the cancellation wasn't 'cause they didn't know whose property was what. They said that Delmar came to Wessler about something that he found by the creek that would make it difficult for him to become the owner of the property and develop it."

"The cemetery," Kyle whispered so that only Lauren could hear.

"I dunno know what it was," said Marva with tears forming in her eyes. "I just know that I told Jefferson about it and he went out there to find what it was that Delmar got on Wessler."

"What time did you tell him all of this?" asked Kyle.

If Marva thought that the question was strange, she didn't let on. "About 6:30. I went straight to his house after work and told him everything."

"That's after he left us," said Lauren. "If he'd known about all of this when he was over at the house, he would have told us."

"So that puts Jefferson out at Coral Road around 7:00," said Kyle. "He was already on the property when we got there."

Lauren's blood ran cold as she remembered something. A car had passed them when they were waiting for Jefferson to arrive.

"I think the shooter drove right past us."

Chapter 31

"We need to get a move on getting that Southside property!" Telly Whitman bellowed into the phone.

"We're working on it," said P.T. Hollingsworth, who was on the other end. "But there's nothing we can do about a cemetery being on the property. How did that dead guy even find out about the cemetery in the first place?"

"LaCrosse was very thorough," Whitmore explained running his hands through his salt and pepper hair. "Especially when it came to the native islanders. He was a pain in the butt to have on staff."

"So the LaCrosse meddler was taken care of. How did the cop find out about it?"

"What cop?!" Whitmore exclaimed.

"The one laid up in the hospital with a gunshot wound to the back. It's all over the news."

"I'll call you back!" Whitmore slammed the phone down and turned on the plasma screen in his study.

"Police Detective, Jefferson Pierce is fighting for his life tonight in the Mainland Hospital after he was gunned down on the Walter Simpson property on Oak Grove Island earlier this evening. The chief of police declined comment as to the reason he was on the property, as it pertains to an open case still under investigation. There is speculation however, that he was out there investigating a cemetery with headstones that interestingly enough date back to the 1800s. We will continue to make reports as we receive updates on Detective Pierce's Condition..."

Whitman turned off the television and sunk his large frame into his leather chair behind his desk. The secret about the cemetery was now public knowledge. Getting that Simpson property now was going to be impossible. There were too many people getting in the way of the plans he had for this island! First, the building inspector and now a police detective. Whitman got up and fixed himself a drink from his wet bar, the ice cubes making a soothing *plunk* as they hit the bottom of the glass.

"It is all so frustrating," he thought angrily. "These people don't know what to do with property! These prime spots are wasting away under their farms and clapboard houses. All of the economic potential for this island is being wasted on an idealistic whim of some dreamers who can't accept progress."

One meddler was taken care of. The other was barely holding on. Would there be more to get out of the way?

Whitman picked up his phone and dialed again.

"It's me," he spoke curtly. "Make it happen…You have? Good! No, under no circumstances are you to do that or you will be sorry!"

Chapter 32

So am I to understand that you two were trespassing on the Simpson property when you found Detective Pierce?" asked the chief at the police station the following morning.

"We weren't aware that anyone still lived on the property," Kyle answered smoothly.

"That doesn't mean you weren't trespassing."

"I saw no signs."

"Uh huh. So what exactly was your business on the Simpson property?"

"We were doing your job," Lauren smart-mouthed. "We were following the leads *you* should have been following –"

"Lauren." Kyle tried to interrupt before she said too much. Even with Jefferson in serious condition, they didn't want to get him into trouble.

"I assume you're talking about the Delmar LaCrosse case?" The chief asked. "Was Detective Pierce following a lead when you found him?"

"We don't know what Jefferson was doing out there," Lauren answered slyly.

"Excuse me, Chief," Kyle spoke up. "But shouldn't you ask us about who we think could have gunned down Detective Pierce in cold blood?"

"Are you trying to do my job for me?" Chief asked peering at the couple over his glasses.

"I wouldn't dream of doing that," said Kyle sarcastically.

"So why don't you answer my question. Was Jefferson working on the Delmar LaCrosse case and were you helping him?"

"That's two questions."

"Besides, he's not a case, he was my cousin," Lauren interrupted. "And you have the wrong people in jail for his murder."

"Who should we have in jail?"

Lauren rolled her eyes. "Look, all I can tell you is that this thing with Delmar is about the land. His murder is much bigger than some robbery. Jefferson was trying to help us out with that and you *suspended* him for it."

"So he was out there because of the LaCrosse case."

Lauren didn't let on that she knew she'd slipped up.

"Like I said, I don't know why Jefferson was there. Unfortunately, he got shot before we could ask him. But I will say that he did try to help us, which is more than I can say for you."

The chief let out a big sigh. "I know," he said. "And I'm going to tell you something. If you tell anyone that I told you this, I will deny it. Suspending Jefferson was my way of protecting him."

"Protecting him, huh? Did a pretty good job with that, didn't you!"

"Anyway," The chief continued ignoring Lauren's sarcasm. "He's very smart and a very dedicated officer. I knew when he brought in Bryce Wessler, he was on to something, but Wessler is a slippery character. He's been mixed up in some things on other islands, in Florida, and out in California. Bad things happen to people who get in his way and each time he's managed to avoid the law."

"What kind of things is he involved in?" Kyle asked.

"Fraud, blackmail, and I suspect foul play in some instances. That's all I'll say. Trust me, the less you know about it, the better."

"Thank you for telling us this much."

"I assume, you're going to pick up where Jefferson left off," Chief concluded.

When Lauren and Kyle didn't answer immediately, the chief spoke. "Look, I admit that we couldn't really do too much for your cousin, Mrs. Malone, but I will need to caution you against continuing this investigation on your own."

"Are you going to continue with it?" Lauren asked smartly.

"We're going to find who shot Jefferson."

"I would start with Wessler," said Kyle. "My wife and I think his car passed us on Coral Road last night."

"We'll check it out. If Jefferson was shot by Wessler, he will pay for it. He may get away with everything else, but he will not get away with shooting one of our own. We *will* nail him for the attempted murder of a police officer."

"That's it?" Lauren asked coldly. "Nothing else? Delmar doesn't get justice for his murder?"

"One step at a time, Mrs. Malone. We think we can get Wessler on attempted murder."

"Now who's not answering questions," Lauren came back at him impatiently. "Will Bryce Wessler answer for Delmar's murder? Yes or no?"

The chief of police looked away from Lauren.

"No I don't believe he will," he said softly.

Chapter 33

"Lauren, I know it's a hard thing to get over, but it would be wise for you to heed the chief's warning about Wessler," John said when the couple returned to the house.

"How can you say that?" Lauren cried. "Don't you care that Delmar won't get justice for his murder?"

John took his daughter's face in his strong hands. "Lauren, Delmar was my nephew. He was my brother's son. My heart aches that he's gone from this earth. I care that some sick person is responsible for the fact that he's not here anymore. But you're here, Lauren. You're my daughter. I love you and I have to protect you. If the chief of police is telling my daughter that even he can't go any further with Delmar's case, then that's saying something big. Lauren, even if you do find proof that is beyond a shadow of a doubt that Wessler murdered Delmar, there are too many things tied up in his death that cannot be touched. Please understand that. You just have to believe that this Wessler monster will get his due at some point in his life."

"And Lauren," Kyle added. "Chief did say they would try to nail Wessler for the attempted murder of a police officer. That's something."

"But that's not for *murder*," Lauren protested. "Unless Jefferson dies which, can still happen."

The latest update when Lauren called Marva at the hospital was that Jefferson was still in a coma, which caused worry from the doctors.

"Well let's pray it doesn't come to that." Then Kyle said, "What's really terrible is that the Rashads are still facing indictment for a murder they didn't even commit."

"Yeah and I bet that's no accident either," Lauren commented off-handedly.

"Baby, they need someone to answer for Delmar."

"But why them?"

"They were there, I suppose," Kyle guessed.

"The Rashads are scapegoats," said John. "The police have to look as if they're doing something. I doubt their case will make it to trial based on the flimsy evidence."

"That's a huge gamble, Daddy" said Lauren. "What if they're convicted?"

Chapter 34

Bryce Wessler slammed the door to the mainland condo he was renting while securing properties on Oak Grove Island. His keys went flying across the solid oak table in the foyer and his jacket barely missed the specially imported mauve colored-armchair in the livingroom.

How dare that backwoods police chief bring him in for questioning? First, that black detective accuses him of killing the building inspector, now the chief is accusing him of shooting the black detective. Bryce went into the library, selected a book, and stared at it.

The Real Key to Success, it read. This was the first time he'd bother to read the title. Bryce opened the book, revealing a cutout where pages should have been. Instead,

The Promise of Palmettos

a black nine millimeter handgun looked up at him menacingly. When he'd taken it from his father's study on his last trip back to Miami, he'd never dreamed he'd actually use it. He'd only brought it for protection from some pretty nasty characters who began recently making his life miserable. Now he would have to get rid of it soon.

If his father knew the trouble he was in this time, he would never let Bryce hear the end of it. Even worse, he would come out of retirement. It had been hard enough for Charles L. Wessler to entrust the company he'd built from the ground up to his only son.

Bryce had proven more than once that he was not his father's son. He lacked ambition and good business sense. Charles had to pull him out of more scrapes then he cared to think about. The latest mistake with the Oak Grove Island deal was positively disastrous, if anyone found out about it, he would be ruined. Fortunately, the Wesslers were able to do major damage control. Then Jefferson Pierce started to poke around. Rather than get his father involved again, Bryce decided to handle it on his own. He didn't think that the police would dare implicate him. The questions that were asked of him this morning had indicated otherwise.

The telephone interrupted Bryce's thoughts.

"Hello," Bryce spoke into the receiver. The book was still in his hands.

"Look Wessler, I've cut you some slack before but you're in deep now."

Bryce recognized the angry voice of P.T. Hollingsworth, a major investor in several of his projects.

"Threatening me isn't going to get you your money any sooner, Hollingsworth. I thought you were on my side."

"I am on your side. Didn't I account for your whereabouts the night that meddler was murdered?"

"I know you did. You did a huge favor because I very well couldn't tell them about Crawford Island."

"You mean how you made off with the deeds to those people's property without paying them the full amount you made the agreement for."

"I couldn't help it if I overspent the budget," Bryce nervously ran his fingers through his long hair.

"And what about that south side property on Oak Grove? You already spent our money and you don't even have the entire property to show for it!" P.T. bellowed. "The fact that your legs are still connected to your body is a good indication of my patience for you and the respect I have for your father. But Bryce, my patience is wearing thin and fast. I'm the only thing that stands between you and the others who put this money in this deal. Come up with our money soon or I'm getting out of the way and whatever happens… happens."

"Oh come on, Hollingsworth," Wessler pleaded.

"And as for your needing an alibi for last night; that is the last favor I do for you. I'm done covering for you. What you did was stupid even for you."

"I know I've messed up. I don't have the money yet but I will."

"I've heard it all before, Bryce."

"I really mean it this time. That thousand acres on the north side of the island will make us a lot of money. If we get that and develop it, you'll have your money and more. That's worth the wait isn't it?"

"What are you going to pay the owners of that north side property with, air?"

"I got it covered."

"Bryce, you've been dealing with them for months now and they have not budged. You've got as much chance of getting those properties as you have winning your father's respect."

Hollingsworth's comments stung but Bryce didn't let him know. He just told him once more that he had it covered. "I also have the thing with that cop handled." Bryce assured Hollingsworth as he stared at the gun.

"You better handle it. You'd better handle all of it because I mean it this time, another screw up and you're worm bait."

Bryce hung up the phone. Though he felt the weight of Hollingsworth's words, there were more pressing matters he needed to tend to. He had to get rid of the gun. The family yacht was docked at the mainland marina. Bryce planned to sail out to the middle of the river and toss the gun overboard. Then there would be nothing to link him to his crimes.

Bryce shoved the gun into his briefcase that was sitting on top of the marble table. He grabbed his keys from the table and swiftly opened the door. Standing before him was a very attractive tall woman. Suddenly, Bryce forgot the urgency of his task.

"What have you got for me?" He asked as the woman breezed past him and headed for the living room.

"Five more properties." She handed him the contracts.

"The beach front?" Bryce asked hopefully as he flipped through them.

"Close. Creekside."

"I need that beach access!" He snapped angrily, trying to keep his feelings of panic under control.

"Patience," she cooed making her way to the wet bar and pouring herself vodka on the rocks. "All in good time."

"You've had time," Bryce tried to get angry but his attraction for her took over. He watched her sit down and licked his lips as she crossed one long, smooth, shapely leg over the other.

"Bryce darling, it's going to take some finesse. It won't be easy getting those properties. Don't worry though," she said patting the spot next to her with her freshly manicured hand. "I've got them right where I want them."

Bryce sat down next to her.

"You did well," he said looking through the deeds. "These are good properties. Most would kill for this commission."

She took a long sip from her glass and set it down on the marble coffee table. Bryce watched her rise to her feet and head for his bedroom, her long dark hair flowing behind her.

Bryce followed and closed the door.

A few hours later, the moonlight filtered through the windows of the condo. The bedside clock read midnight. The clandestine meeting came to an abrupt end and wrinkled clothes were thrown on hastily. There were no goodbye kisses, just promises for more business dealings in the future. Now more urgent matters needed to be addressed. Bryce hopped into his black Jaguar XK8 and the woman in her white Ford Explorer, each speeding off in different directions.

Chapter 35

"Hey babe, whatcha doing?" Kyle asked coming into the bedroom.

Lauren was sitting in bed, flipping through the pages that she was holding. "I'm looking for the jerk that ran me off the road. Maybe if they're connected to Wessler, the police will reopen Delmar's case."

Kyle shut the door behind him. "Lauren, do you really want to keep putting yourself through this?"

"Put myself through what? Getting justice for my murdered cousin?"

"Do you really think Wessler hired someone?"

"Yes, I do," she responded as she flipped through another page.

"Lauren, there are a million possibilities on who could have run you off the road and they may not be registered in this county or even in this state. Remember, Wessler is from Florida."

"Then I'll look up the SUVs registered in Florida," she responded and flipped another page.

Kyle didn't know how he could make his wife see reason.

"And I did some research," said Lauren still reading through the listings. "Did you know that the cemetery we found out by the creek has union soldiers buried there? Marva called to tell me that she found out that Delmar was researching a way to get the property turned into a historical landmark so that Wessler couldn't get it. If that's not a motive to kill him, I don't know what is. I think we should go to the chief with this, Kyle."

"Lauren," Kyle said softly as he placed his hand on top of hers. "It's over. We came to Oak Grove to find out who killed your cousin and we did. I am so sorry that Delmar won't get the justice that he's entitled to, but there's nothing more we can do. It's time to go home. Justin is waiting on his mama to come back to him. Don't you miss him?"

Lauren took her hand away and began flipping through the pages again. "Of course I miss him."

"Then let's not obsess over something we can't do anything about and focus on raising him."

Lauren threw the papers to the side and got out of the bed. She began to gather up the clothes that had been lying around the room over chairs and on doorknobs.

"Lauren what are you doing?" Kyle asked rubbing his fingers over his temples.

"I'm packing," she could not disguise the crack in her voice. "We're going home tomorrow, aren't we? Then we need to pack our stuff."

"Do you want help?"

"Nope," Lauren said curtly.

"Okay," Kyle said softly without taking his eyes off her.

Lauren knew that she was being unreasonable but she didn't care. She was angry at the world right now. She was angry at Wessler for being rich and powerful enough to get away with murder. She was angry at the police for being cowards. And right then, although it wasn't fair, she was the angriest at Kyle for not being as angry as she was.

Lauren grabbed her purses and one by one, throwing them into the suitcase. When she spotted her black purse, the one with the broken strap, she was torn as to whether or not she should just discard it. Deciding that it could be fixed, Lauren picked it up from the floor and heard a strange clinking noise from deep inside. It sounded like something was broken. She checked the first compartment where she usually kept her wallet and checkbook when she carried it, but it was empty. In the second compartment, Lauren found large shards of glass but she couldn't figure out what it was. Carefully emptying her purse, she pulled out a broken picture frame. It was the picture that Granddad took of her, Delmar, and Netta. It took Lauren a moment to remember how it ended up in her purse. She had been carrying this purse the night she was chased out of Delmar's apartment. In her haste to get away, Lauren must have stuffed the picture, frame and all, into her purse and forgotten about it.

Lauren looked over at Kyle but he'd busied himself with flipping through the channels on the television and settled on a *Seinfeld* rerun. He was totally absorbed in the episode that happened to be one of his favorites, when he was startled by the sound of something crashing against the wall. In a sudden burst of renewed frustration when she'd seen the picture, Lauren had let the picture fly. Kyle watched his wife for a moment, who was on the floor crying. Then he went over, picked up the picture in its broken frame and brought it to Lauren.

"Don't throw away your memories, Sweetie," Kyle said gently.

Lauren clutched the photograph and the frame. As she leaned against Kyle, she caught a shiny glint that made her look down.

"Hey there is something on the back of this frame."

"What is it?"

Lauren turned the frame over to show Kyle. Tape onto the back was a key and a slip of paper with the words *Island Savings Bank, Box 24.*

Chapter 36

"Bryce Wessler! Open up, we've got a search warrant!"

A sleepy and very disheveled Bryce opened the door, letting in what looked to be the entire police department. The search of the entire condominium took two hours. Rubber gloved hands touched every surface, upturned every cushion, fumbled through every drawer, and flipped through every book. They even checked the door and the window frames. When all was said and done, the police held onto two plastic baggies. One held the fake book, *The Real Key to Success*. The other baggie held a pair of muddy, expensive shoes. A white t-shirt and silk pajama-bottomed, Bryce Wessler was escorted from his condo, hands cuffed behind him, arrested for the suspicion of attempted murder of Detective Jefferson Pierce.

Chapter 37

With a trembling hand, Lauren reached into her purse, pulled out the silver key, and handed it to Delmar's mother.

"Aunt Dinah, I found this key taped behind a picture frame in Delmar's apartment. We believe that the key opens a safe deposit box at the Island Savings Bank."

Dinah LaCrosse reached for the key. Her other hand covered her mouth, keeping in the sobs that threatened to escape at any moment. It seemed that all she'd been able to do over the past few weeks is cry. She hadn't the strength to do anything else. Not be a wife. Not be a mother to her two remaining children. Not cook. Not clean. Just cry and ask the question, "why?" She knew that the key her niece was handing to her held the answers. Lauren had done something that neither she nor her husband had the strength to do: Find the answers. Now again, she felt devoid of all strength as she reached for the key.

"No," said Dinah and let her hand drop.

"It's yours, Aunt Dinah. Delmar went through great lengths to hide this. We owe it to him to find out the real reason he died. We might not find justice, but at least it will help us find peace."

"Lauren," Dinah let out a shuddering sigh. "You've been here for weeks searching for the truth. You've come this far. It's up to you to find the rest of the truth. So you take that key and…" Dinah's voice began to falter, but she finished her sentence. "…and you find out what my baby had to tell us."

Chapter 38

"Lauren, I need you to realize that it's not going to be easy to access Delmar's safe deposit box," said Kyle as the two of them drove to the mainland.

"What are you talking about?" Lauren was trying to contain her excitement of finding the piece of the puzzle that could put an end to the mystery, so she wasn't completely processing what Kyle was trying to tell her.

"I'm saying that you aren't going to just be able to stroll into the bank, produce the key and that will be enough to get into the safe deposit box."

"Why wouldn't they let me in?" Lauren asked with alarm. "I'm family."

"It doesn't matter. Only a co-owner of the box, an appointed guardian, or one with power of attorney, who has specific permission, can get access to the box. Safe deposit boxes are great for keeping things safe, but sometimes things are kept too safe and heirs can't get to what's inside."

"Do you mean to tell me that whatever is in Delmar's box is trapped forever?"

"Not forever. They'll remove the contents once they determine the box inactive."

"How long will that take?"

"No telling."

"Kyle what are we going to do?" Lauren was frustrated. How could they be so close and so far at the same time?

"We've got to get into that box, Kyle," Lauren said with that determined tone in her voice.

"How? Those who have access to the box initially had to sign their name in the presence of the bank. Each time the box is visited, their signatures are verified. That's even before you get to the vault."

"What happens in the vault?"

"The box is opened with two keys," Kyle explained. "The owner has a key and the bank has a master key. The box will not unlock unless both keys are inserted."

It all reminded Lauren of the movie, *Mission Impossible.*

"How do you know all of this?"

"You remember the guy I worked with on that downtown development, Chad Meyer?"

"Vaguely."

"His father passed suddenly leaving a safe deposit box with just the key and no power of attorney. The family had to wait until they emptied the box. They were only able to recover their valuables when they were threatened to be auctioned off five years later."

"Five years! I am not waiting five years to get into this box, Kyle!" Lauren exclaimed. "Besides, who's going to auction off a bunch of papers?"

"Assuming he's got just papers in there."

"What else would it be?"

"That's the thing about safe deposit boxes," said Kyle as he turned into the small parking lot of the Island Savings Bank. "Only Delmar knows what he put in it."

"If it's so hopeless, then why are we still going into the bank?"

"Because I've got a plan."

Chapter 39

"Before I issue you your keys, please read over the terms and conditions for the box rental, then sign at the bottom," drawled a middle-aged blond woman sitting behind a huge oak desk.

The name Mrs. Minerva was etched into a gold name plate on her desk. She handed the couple the papers, which Kyle took and began to read. When he was finished signing his name in that squiggly scrawl that he was so proud of, he glanced at Lauren as if to say, *This is what I expected.*

Lauren took her turn reading the agreement. It was exactly as Kyle explained. She came to the part about missed payments and confiscation of contents. If Kyle's plan didn't work, they might never see what Delmar had hidden. Lauren drew in a quick breath and signed the paper.

"Down here in the vault room is where we keep the safe deposit boxes," Mrs. Minerva led them into a room that barely held the three of them.

Lauren hoped that Mrs. Minerva wasn't too bright and they could get away with pulling off this heist.

"Now those keys you have are the only two keys for your box. If you lose them, tell us immediately and we will get you a new box, but you'll need to pay a $150 fee."

"Why so much?" Lauren asked with surprise. Furtively, she scoped out the location of the security cameras and the order of the boxes.

"Because the bank does not keep a spare key to your box. The box would have to be drilled open and the locks replaced. That's how seriously we take security."

"I see," Lauren responded trying to keep the nervousness out of her voice.

"Now the key I have is the bank's master key. Your box will not open with just your key and it will not open with just my key. Both keys will need to be in the lock."

Mrs. Minerva pulled her key ring off of her wrist and put the key in the lock of box 17. So far, it was working out in their favor. The couple had lucked out with the box numbers. Lauren pulled out her key and fumbled for the lock. The key fell from her sweaty hands and landed by Mrs. Minerva's foot.

"Oh let me –!" Mrs. Minerva reached down for the key. Kyle, being the gentleman he was, also reached for the key and –

"Ow!"

Kyle and Mrs. Minerva bumped heads hard. Kyle, ignoring the throbbing pain in his own head, immediately came to Mrs. Minerva's aid. "Are you alright? I am so sorry!" He held onto Mrs. Minerva while she was doubled over clutching her head.

"Let's me see it." Kyle tried to pry her hands away to inspect the wound.

"I'm okay, Mr. Malone." Mrs. Minerva answered shakily as she tried to see past the stars that she was seeing.

Kyle looked over the banker's shoulder at Lauren who, being mindful of the security camera, blocked what she was doing with her body. Reaching behind her, she quietly slipped the master key out of box 17 and just as quietly slid it into the lock of box 24.

"Should I get someone?" Kyle asked still trying to steady the poor woman who looked to be on the verge of toppling over.

"Oh that won't be necessary," said Mrs. Minerva slowly straightening up.

Lauren asked concerned, "Are you sure you're alright?"

"I'm fine. Here's your key, Mrs. Malone."

Mrs. Minerva handed Lauren what she thought was her key, but it was actually Delmar's key. During the trip down to the safe deposit box, Lauren had made the switch. The Malones' actual key was safely in the bottom of her purse.

Lauren stuck the key into box 24. Mrs. Minerva turned her key in the first lock. Lauren turned her key in the second lock. Mrs. Minerva swung the door open, pulled out the box, and carried it into the viewing room next door. To ensure privacy, this room had no cameras.

"I'll be just outside this door when you get finished," said Mrs. Minerva. "Take as much time as you need."

"Thank you," said Lauren barely daring to breath.

"Thank you, Mrs. Minerva," said Kyle. "Sorry again about your head."

No sooner than the door had closed Lauren lifted the lid off the box.

"Take everything out of the box," Kyle whispered urgently. "We'll sort through it later."

Lauren stuffed a stack of papers and a large envelope into her purse. Good thing she brought a large one.

Moments later, the Malones walked swiftly to the car, not believing they pulled the whole thing off.

Chapter 40

The couple ran into the house, straight into the family room and closed the door.

"I cannot believe you head-butted the woman!" exclaiming Lauren finally having the courage to speak now they were in the safety of the house.

"It was an accident," laughed Kyle. "I didn't know you were going to drop the key. You were supposed to tell her that your key didn't fit then trick the woman into believing that she'd gotten the wrong box number."

"I didn't mean to drop the key, but once I did and you practically knocked Mrs. Minerva out, I had a plan that I thought would work out better," said Lauren. "I was really nervous about trying to pull off our original plan."

"You're lucky that worked, Lauren," Kyle said now serious. "Some banks have an original key for each box. Good thing that particular bank uses a master key."

Lauren swallowed the lump that suddenly formed in her throat. She hadn't thought about that. They could have been behind bars right now, if they'd been caught. The important thing is that they got what they came for.

Lauren carefully removed the papers and the envelope from her purse and placed them on the ottoman.

"I thought that there would be more than this," said Lauren.

"Well let's see what he's got," said Kyle reaching for one of the papers. "It must be really important if he kept it all locked away."

Lauren picked up a document also. "This looks like a rezoning report. He's got a complete description of the property; the current owner, which is Wessler-Forest of course; and a photograph of the property.

"It looks like stuff we managed to find out on our own."

"Even still, it's good to know that we were on the right track. At least he was smart enough to lock it all away.

"What's in the envelope?" asked Kyle.

Lauren picked up the manila envelope and opened the flap. She emptied the contents out onto the table. It was a VHS tape.

Lauren asked, "What do you suppose this is?"

"Why don't you pop it into the VCR and find out," said Kyle.

Lauren stuck the tape in and turned on the television. Instantly Delmar was on the screen standing in front of the big oak on Grandma Henrietta's property. Lauren almost cried out loud when she heard his voice. It was like he was in the room with him.

"If you're watching this tape right now, then something bad must have really happened and my resourceful cousin, Lauren found a way to get into my safe-deposit box. Just kidding. Mostly."

Lauren let out a chuckle through her tears.

"I kept records of everything that was going on, because I thought that someday people on this island needed to know the truth about what really happened to it. What I am about to say is very difficult but here goes. Oak Grove Island is under siege by some very powerful people. You probably know by now that the Wessler-Forest Corporation is taking over to turn the island into an expensive paradise. You can forget about booking a reservation folks, because our people are not invited. Almost every piece of property on this island has been earmarked for development.

Councilman Telly Whitman is spearheading this development in a push to become mayor of an island that our people would no longer recognize. What you may not know is that according to the other council members, Whitman has been leaning on them to pass the rezonings that I recommend for denial. He has gone so far as to threaten their families, get powerful people to raise their taxes, and other horrible things.

They could not pass the rezoning last night because they miscalculated the property line. Bryce Wessler was in my office this morning to file a rezoning appeal pending a survey of the parcel in question. If he is allowed to rezone this property, there will already be over 1000 acres of uninterrupted development. For now, I was able to stop Wessler from developing the piece adjacent to the Walter Simpson Property because I discovered a two-acre cemetery, next to Blue Creek. Unfortunately for Wessler, it sits in the middle of his would be conservation subdivision. The National Register of Historic Places is very interested in this cemetery and a temporary injunction has been placed against development. Wessler let me know in no uncertain terms that he was unhappy with me and told me to 'watch my back'."

Lauren and Kyle exchanged astonished glances.

"If you found my box, then you found supporting documents that highlight the specific properties this corporation is targeting. These are the most valuable properties on the island. The LaCrosse properties belonging to Grandma Henrietta and Aunt Eleanor are at the top of the list. The old Walter Simpson property, which is the property that Wessler miscalculated, is also a much desired piece. Fortunately, the only remaining Simpson heir has refused to sell."

Lauren paused the tape. "No wonder Delmar was a target. Do you suppose if we give this tape to the police, it will be enough to arrest Wessler for murder?"

"I don't know, Lauren. The chief made it pretty damn clear that they were finished with Delmar's case," said Kyle. "On the plus side, they did arrest Wessler this morning for shooting Jefferson."

"*What? When?* Why are you now just telling me this?"

"They got him this morning. It was on the news while you were over at Aunt Dinah's. Then we got busy at the bank

"Okay, you're forgiven," said Lauren. "But attempted murder isn't the same as actual murder."

"I know, Sweetie, but it's better than nothing."

"I hope Delmar sees it that way," Lauren sighed and restarted the tape.

Delmar continued to go into complete detail confirming everything that Lauren and Kyle had already found out.

Then Delmar said with a very sad expression, "There are other things that are happening that you will unfortunately have to find out for yourselves. Please when you find out try to be understanding and forgiving. And to Lauren, my dear blood cousin, take care of Netta. I know she can be hard to love sometimes but she really needs you. Most importantly, you need to sit down with Grandma Henrietta and have a talk with her. Tell her that I told you to and she'll give some leverage that you hopefully won't need. Remember the promise we made to Granddad Lazarus. We won't be able to stop what's happening, but we can protect ourselves. Lauren, I knew that you would find a way to my box no matter what. I knew it was a long shot putting it behind our picture, but it was the only place I could think of to hide it without the wrong people finding it. As much as they lead you to believe it, Island Bank ain't no Fort Knox."

Lauren chuckled again.

"Mom and Dad, I love you. I'm sorry that it turned out like this but just know that I'm okay and I that I had to do this. When I became a planner, I swore that I would protect my land, my heritage, and my people. Or die trying. I love every one of you. Take care of yourselves. Most importantly, hold onto the land and to each other."

The screen faded to black and Kyle turned off the tape.

"How do you feel?" Kyle asked Lauren.

She answered with her eyes surprisingly dry, "Overwhelmed. When I saw that it was a tape of Delmar, I thought he would answer some things, but now I have more questions than answers."

"That's something about Councilman Whitman, huh?"

"We knew that the man was serious about becoming mayor but he's bold to actually threaten the council members. Why didn't they report it?"

Kyle answered, "Probably for the same reasons they voted with him to push through the rezonings. They were scared."

"What do you suppose Delmar wanted us to find out for ourselves? Why didn't he just come out and say what it was?"

"I don't know," Kyle answered. "Maybe he didn't want to be the one to spread that kind of hurt."

Lauren sighed. "Yeah, he never did like to talk about people no matter what they'd done.

"So are you going to see Grandma before we leave this afternoon?" Kyle asked.

"I have to. Like I said, I have more questions," said Lauren reaching for the papers that came from the safe deposit box. "Let's see what the rest of these papers say. Oh my goodness!"

"What is it?"

"This is a photograph that Delmar had taken of one of the properties up for rezoning. Look what happened to get caught up in the shot?"

Lauren handed Kyle the papers. Rubbing his hand over his goatee he said, "Hmm, looks like we found your white van."

"Yep," Lauren responded curtly.

"Del really got a good shot of the side."

"Yep."

"Guess you should have looked under commercial licensing."

"Yep."

"What are you going to do about it?" Kyle asked surprised at how calm Lauren was considering what she was looking at.

He handed her back the document.

"Nothing. As of now, I am officially *done*."

With that said Lauren laid the incriminating evidence to the side and reached for another document.

"Okay, this one is a rezoning of the south side property," said Lauren flipping through the pages. Suddenly, she got extremely excited, "Kyle! You are not going to believe this!"

"I'm still trying to get over the last thing. What else could you possibly find?"

When Delmar found out about that Wessler-Forest miscalculated the property lines for the south side property, he did a property search."

"Yeah, it's Walter Simpson's property, remember? Except he's dead so I suppose it belongs to his daughter."

"Yes, right. But guess who's the daughter?"

"Who?"

"Deanna Simpson Rashad."

"Rashad?" Kyle tried to place the name. "Rashad! The same Rashad that's in jail now because they couldn't raise the bail money?!"

"That's them. It would be very convenient for the police to pin Delmar's murder on them. If the Rashads are convicted, they could stand to lose that property seeing that she's the last surviving heir. There would be no one to pay the property taxes. They would have no choice but to sell the land."

"Or they would have to put the land up as bail," Kyle pointed out.

"Dang, wiped both ways," Lauren commented, scarcely able to believe it. "I wonder if the police realize this is what is going on?"

"It's the perfect crime," Kyle said with astonishment. "They kill Delmar who has enough information to nail all of these bigwigs, then turn right around and pin it on the owners of the property that they want for the murder."

Chapter 41

Based on the evidence you've presented us with, there's enough to bring in Telly Whitman for questioning, although I'm not sure it's going to do any good," the Chief of Police said to Lauren and Kyle when they arrived at the precinct forty-five minutes later.

"Why not?" asked Lauren who was already irritated. The chief told them after viewing the tape that he refused to touch Wessler as it related to Delmar LaCrosse. It concerned property that too many powerful people wanted and to pursue it would be pure suicide. They had Wessler on attempted murder, and that was the best he could do. The chief refused to discuss it further. Lauren and Kyle exchanged glances. If the police were being leaned on, the chief was doing a good job to keep it under wraps."

"Unless you're able to get the council members to corroborate Delmar's accusation," the chief was saying, "it's just one man's word over another."

"Well can you at least question him?" Kyle asked frustrated. Getting justice for this land scandal was like pulling teeth.

"I could," chief answered slowly. "But I doubt it would do any good. See a lot of the council members are native islanders who are easily threatened by a man as powerful as Telly Whitman."

"Are you saying that native islanders are too weak to stand up for themselves?" Lauren asked insulted.

"No," said the chief realizing his statement came out wrong. "I'm saying that the people on this island feel they have a lot to lose when going up against someone as powerful as Whitman. They can lose their land, their family, and their lives even. For people living in an isolated community such as this, life is simple. They fish, they farm, they spend time with their families, and they go to church. These things mean a lot to people on this island, especially for the older folks. They want to maintain that life and Whitman is threatening it. The younger people don't quite understand and are the ones who are selling their family's land. When they cross the bridge to the mainland, they'll find that life is busier, colder, and money is more important than having values."

"Chief, you're making my point. If the council stops Whitman, they can save that way of life they want to protect."

"They can't save everyone," the chief said quietly. "They can only protect themselves."

Lauren was quiet. The police chief was saying everything her father had been saying to her ever since she found out about the land being sold off. So did her mother. Aunt Eleanor told her the same thing in the store parking lot. Even Delmar said it on the tape he'd made.

Selling property was the choice of the individual. If they decided to sell, there was little she could do about it. All she could do is make sure her family held onto what they had. Now it was her turn to make sure that the next generation, which included her son, Justin, understood that the land was worth more than any amount of money offered.

"What's going to happen to the Rashads?" asked Lauren moving on to a new subject.

"They'll have to stand trial. But I will see that their lawyer is made aware of their connection to the property coveted by Mr. Wessler."

Kyle stood up and Lauren followed suit.

"Thank you for your time, Chief."

"No, thank *you*," said the chief. "We will definitely question Councilman Whitman about his activities on the council."

The Malones turned to leave. Lauren turned back to the chief and said, "Chief, with all of this questioning you're doing, aren't you tired of not getting any answers?"

Chapter 42

Lauren ran her hands along the thick, strong-branches of the mighty oak tree.

"I am always amazed at how beautiful this tree is," said Kyle. "You don't see oaks like this anywhere but here."

Lauren didn't answer. Her eyes had fallen on the spot of the bark that was stained red by Delmar's and her blood years ago.

"After all of this time, I can't believe it's still here," Lauren whispered.

Kyle looked at the spot also. "This is where you and Delmar became blood cousins?"

"Yeah," said Lauren, hopping up on one of the low branches, taking care not to tear her flowered skirt. "We need to take Justin out to this tree. Maybe one day he'll play out here with his cousins."

"Maybe he will," said Kyle with a grin. "Are you ready to see your grandmother now?"

"I am," said Lauren jumping down. "But I'm also afraid of what she has to tell me."

"I'll be with you the whole time," said Kyle extending his hand to Lauren. She took it and the two of them walked towards the house.

Grandma Henrietta smiled when she saw her grandchildren.

"Come on in," she said holding open the screen door for them.

"I saw your father earlier," said Grandma when the three of them had taken a seat. "He said that you were leaving today."

"Yes. We're leaving in a few hours, Grandma," said Lauren looking around the living room.

She'd been in this room many times throughout her life, but she looked as if she were seeing it for the first time. Every last child, grandchild, and great-grandchild had a picture on the shelves, the walls, and the fire place mantle. There had to be over a hundred photographs in that room. Baby pictures, school pictures, graduation and wedding photos, and photos just because. The photographs were a timeline of achievements for each LaCrosse. But they were more than just photographs. It was a representation of a strong and proud family. The huge portrait of Henrietta and Lazarus stared down at all of them. Then Lauren spied the smiling picture of Delmar and was suddenly aware of his presence. He was gone from this world but his spirit was still in the room and in their hearts.

Lauren had almost lost her courage to ask her grandmother to put into place the final piece of this puzzle. But being surrounded by the people she loved and those who loved her, she found the strength to ask her question.

"Grandmama, before Kyle and I leave today, there is something that I need to ask you."

"What is it?" Henrietta asked looking at her intently. She reminded Lauren of her father who had the tendency to give that exact same facial expression. It was as if she could see straight through her.

"This isn't going to be easy, but Delmar gave me a message in some stuff of his that we found. He asked me to ask you to tell me what you told him."

"He did, did he?" Henrietta looked as if she had been expecting this question. She did not speak for a very long while and Lauren sat patiently waiting. When Henrietta finally said something, Lauren had to strain to hear her.

"I'm not sure that I should tell you."

"Why not, Grandma?" Lauren asked gently taking her hand.

"Because I don't want to lose you too."

"You won't lose me," Lauren assured her.

"How do I know that?" Henrietta cried out. "I told my grandson, and he's dead."

"And you think what you told him got him killed?" Lauren asked gently. "Is that why you screamed out at Delmar's funeral?"

Henrietta nodded with tears streaming down her face. Kyle left the room to search for a Kleenex. He came back and handed some to her.

"Grandma, I'm not going to let anything happen to Lauren," said Kyle. "Delmar asked you to tell Lauren, so we have to believe that what you have to say is important. You can't keep it a secret."

"Does Dad know the secret?" asked Lauren.

Henrietta shook her head. "The only people who know..." her words trailed off. Lauren did not need for her grandmother to finish that sentence to understand that besides herself, the only people who knew this secret had passed on.

Henrietta cleared her throat and began her story with a strong voice.

"Lazarus and Micah were as close as two brothers could get. Their grandparents settled this land after the civil war. LaCrosse property was the entire northern tip of this island. Right where that old oak is, the one where you and Delmar used to play, used to be the front yard of the original LaCrosse home until the storm took it in 1955."

"I didn't know that," Lauren said.

"Yes it was. Your great-grandfather, Samuel knew he couldn't live forever so he never rebuilt the house. Instead, he wanted to make sure that his land would get to his two sons with no problem after he died. He'd seen too many families squabble over land ownership. So he went to the tax office and made sure that the LaCrosse property was split into equal halves and given to his sons. Lazarus got the beachside and Micah, the riverside. The creek formed the dividing line. Up until his death, Samuel lived with us and our nine children in the new house Lazarus had built for his family. And you know that your great-grandmother, Nadine died when Lazarus and Micah were small.

So for many years, we lived on our respective properties, farming the land and fishing in the waters. We worked hard. And we were all close. We had Sunday dinners at each other's houses and our kids played together, although Micah and Eleanor raised a rowdy bunch. Maybe that's what drove Micah to an early grave. He was a soft-spoken and gentle man, but Eleanor was hard and the kids were hard. Except for the daughter. Ellen was the only one of them who amounted to anything. But them other kids were constantly getting into trouble. Junior was always getting arrested. Torrin, that's Netta's father, was hanging around that rough crowd and they was always sellin' drugs.

Micah probably aged 50 years tryin' to keep them fools out of trouble. Then in 1979, Torrin went and did it. He and that no-good wife of his, Eliza. They got busted in a huge sting and to bail them out of jail took more than Micah and Eleanor had. Micah was ready to wash his hands of him but Eleanor wouldn't have it, so Micah did the only thing he could. He offered to sell Lazarus his half of the land. Lazarus understood his brother was proud and would never go to anyone else with this. Plus it was just as important to Micah to keep the land in the family, so Lazarus accepted the deal."

"You mean –?" Lauren started to interrupt.

"Let me finish, Baby. They wrote out the terms, an unrecorded deed I think it's called, and attached one of those promised notes saying that Micah could buy back the property when he got on his feet again. But Micah and his family could continue to live on the property as if the deal hadn't been made. Then Lazarus locked the deed away somewhere safe. Your grandfather told me about the deal as soon as it was struck, but Eleanor never knew. She would have had Micah's head if she found out that she was indebted to us."

"Did Uncle Micah ever pay back Granddad?" Lauren asked, barely able to speak from the shock of what her grandmother was telling her.

"No, he died before that could happen and when my sweet Lazarus died, I thought I would let the secret die with him. I didn't see the need in claiming the property and Eleanor certainly didn't need to know that I owned all of it. And for years, I kept it quiet, even from my kids. The deed remained locked in a safe deposit box that I opened with Lazarus at the Island Bank. I almost forgot about it until a few months ago."

"What made you remember the deed, Grandma?" Lauren prompted her. This must have been the difficult part of Henrietta's story because her breathing came in shallow breaths.

"Delmar went out to Eleanor's because he found out about the developers wanting the LaCrosse land. First he came to warn me, but he needn't have worried because I wasn't selling. Then he went over to Eleanor's. He knocked at the front door but there was no answer. Then he heard voices coming from the back porch. Delmar stood right there and heard Eleanor and Netta fight over selling the land."

"Let me guess," Lauren said bitterly. "Netta wanted to sell it for Eleanor and Eleanor didn't want to sell her land. Oh yeah right, she wasn't going to break her promise to Granddad."

"You got the first part right. Netta wanted to sell the property for Eleanor because they were offering at least 250 million for her property."

Kyle whistled. "With that commission, Netta would stand to make 15 million dollars."

Lauren gave Kyle a look. She bet any amount of money that this is what Delmar meant in his tape. Delmar must have known that Lauren would never understand nor forgive Netta for her betrayal. After the latest stunt Netta pulled, she had already crossed the line with Lauren. She was at the point where nothing Netta did surprised her anymore. Nevertheless, Lauren was still angry.

"That greedy little –!"

"Lauren," Kyle warned her that she was in the presence of her grandmother.

Henrietta continued as if her granddaughter wasn't close to cussing out her cousin. "Eleanor wasn't stupid. She knew Netta would make commission and refused to let her sell it for her because she wanted to sell it herself."

"Well now I know why Netta was pissed off with Eleanor for not selling her any land," Lauren commented. "Even having a small portion, Netta could have had the power to sell it outright and make a lot of money."

"And the developers promised Eleanor an even 300 million if she could convince me to sell my property.

"So what did Delmar do when he heard all of this?"

"He ran to tell me of course. He came here totally distraught. Delmar felt like he let Lazarus down because of the promise he made to him not to sell the land."

"Del and I took the promise very seriously," said Lauren. "I guess Netta was just telling Granddad what he wanted to hear."

"I told Delmar not to worry," Henrietta continued. "And I told him about the deed at the Island Bank. Delmar was concerned about the safety of the deed because the bank security isn't all it should be."

Kyle and Lauren exchanged knowing looks.

"So we met in Atlanta –"

"Is that why Delmar was on his way to Atlanta the last day I saw him?"

"Yes," said Grandma sadly. "We went separately as to not arouse suspicion and we opened up a safe deposit box. I made him the agent in case of an emergency.

"And now that the agent is deceased, you need a new one," said Kyle. "That's why Delmar wanted Lauren to come and see you. He knew that his life was in danger."

"Grandma, are you willing to fight Eleanor to keep this land?"

"Yes I am." Henrietta was resolute. "This is LaCrosse land and it's going to stay LaCrosse land. If I have to snatch back Eleanor's land in order for her not to sell it, then I will surely do that."

Lauren slowly asked her grandmother, "Does she know about the deed now?"

"I don't know." Henrietta began to cry again. "But my grandson is dead and I have this feeling in the pit of my stomach that *someone* found out about it."

Chapter 43

"The day we buried Delmar, Eleanor came to see me," continued Henrietta.

"I saw her go into your bedroom," Lauren remembered. "What did she want?"

"She told me that whatever I thought I had over her wouldn't hold up in court and to give up thinking I was doing anyone any good by keeping this land."

"It sounds like she knows something," said Kyle.

"But what would her knowing about the land have to do with Delmar?" asked Lauren.

"What if he confronted Eleanor with the information?" Kyle alleged. "If Delmar was serious about keeping the land in the family, I wouldn't put it past him to let Eleanor know that the land is not hers to sell."

"But to kill Delmar?" Lauren could barely conceive the notion. "What would that accomplish?"

"With Delmar out of the way, the secret is safe."

"It's Grandma's secret though. Why would she just harm Delmar?"

"That's a good point," Kyle sighed defeated. "So it looks like we're back to accusing Wessler."

Chapter 44

Wessler sank back into his couch made of imported European leather. It was good to be home. Thanks to his father's influence, he was arraigned quickly. Bail of a million dollars was paid – somehow Dan Dansbury convinced the judge he wasn't a flight risk – and Bryce Wessler was sent home after being detained for one night.

Wessler jumped up from where he was sitting. He had work to do. It was time to finish up his deals and get out of Oak Grove immediately. The investors were getting impatient with him and were sniffing for blood.

Wessler headed for the spacious bedroom and began to pull clothes out of the closet and drawers. He was in the middle of stuffing an Italian suit into a garment bag when he heard a knock at the door. He hoped it was her. She only had a couple of more deals to secure and then he could leave this place. She had assured Wessler that she was close to tying up all of the loose ends.

Wessler opened the door and she breezed in.

"What do you have for me?" Wessler asked expectantly.

"All done," she replied, handing him the contracts.

"Really?" Wessler took the contracts from her. "You did it?"

"Going somewhere?" She had looked past his shoulder to see his clothes sprawled out everywhere.

"I've got some deals to make in other places."

"I'll come with you," she said putting her arms around Wessler.

"Later. I need you here to make sure everything goes smoothly. I still want that beach property."

"Told you. I've got it covered," she leaned in to kiss him. Bryce Wessler kissed her back hungrily.

"What the hell is this?" Demanded a very angry voice.

She and Wessler turned towards the door to the condo they had left open.

"Netta, I can explain," Wessler started.

"You better explain something!" Netta shouted.

"It just happened."

"I risked my marriage to be with you!" Netta charged at Bryce, who had let go of the woman, and cowered under Netta's fury.

"Ronnie and I –"

"Oh yes, Ronnie Tremaine," Netta turned on the woman. "Aren't you supposed to be sitting behind the desk at the office answering my phones?"

Ronnie backed up behind Bryce.

"How could you do this?" Netta pushed Bryce hard and the papers he was holding went flying.

Netta bent down to pick them up. As she read them, the expression on her face grew angrier.

"You gave the contracts to *her*?" Netta exploded. "ALS Realty is *my* business! Why would you give them to Ronnie?!"

Bryce's expression grew from fearful to cold.

"You thought I would trust you to sell my million dollar developments?"

"Why wouldn't you? You trusted me to get the rest of the land for you! I talked people into selling land that's been in their family for generations!"

"Yes you did, but you didn't get the LaCrosse property like I wanted."

"I told you about that! Eleanor will sell directly to you but Henrietta won't even consider it. Eleanor's talked to her. *Hell*, I've talked to her!"

"Yeah and your cousin, Delmar also talked to Henrietta!" Wessler yelled. "He overheard your conversation about the deal I made with Eleanor and he told Henrietta."

"How do you know that?" Netta demanded to know.

"He confronted me with it!" Bryce yelled. "That little piss ant was a real headache for me."

Netta glowered at him. "Did you kill my cousin?"

"No, but someone sure did me a favor,"

Bryce stumbled over from the fierce blow Netta just landed on the right side of his face.

"Look, I hooked up with you because I wanted the LaCrosse property. You couldn't get that for me, so I don't need you anymore," said Bryce picking himself off the couch and rubbed his jaw.

"You used me."

"Hey, you're not exactly innocent here. You made lots of money off of your so-called people, Netta."

"I was good enough to buy up the land for you but not to sell the properties?"

Bryce scoffed. "You think I would let a little Geechee girl sell my properties to my investors? Get real. They would never buy it."

"This Geechee girl was good enough to have in your bed."

"Well about that: I was just curious. Tell your husband he's a lucky man."

Netta went to hit him again, but Bryce grabbed her arm. "Behave yourself, Netta."

She wrenched her arm free from his grasp.

"Why does Ronnie get the contracts? She's just my secretary."

"I have had my license for a month," Ronnie said haughtily. She was braver now that she knew that Bryce was on her side.

"Why didn't you just go to Bryce yourself? Why infiltrate my business?"

"You had the in, Netta. You know the islanders so they have your trust. They would sell their land to you without blinking. But I knew that's not where the real money was. I want to sell the developments once they were built. Working with you, I had access to your files so I knew where the new projects were going. Then I let Wessler know that I was available and capable of making him a lot of money. I've sold 75% of the new development and counting." Ronnie sashayed over to the couch and crossed one very long leg over the other. "The rest is history."

Netta just laughed. This was something! If she had been able to be the agent for Bryce's development, she would have had profits coming in for years.

Netta looked at this white woman with her green eyes, long dark hair, and olive skin. She felt in that instant like nothing. This woman did none of the hard work and yet she was reaping the rewards just because she was the right color and had legs that went on forever. Netta had built her company from the ground up. Put every cent she had into ensuring its success. In trying to achieve that success, Netta sold out her family, her own people, and herself. All that to become a millionaire so that her children would have the options she never had living with Eleanor all of those years. Now she wondered if any of it was worth the pain she'd just gone through.

Netta didn't say anything else. She knew she had been beaten. Grabbing her purse, she stormed out of the condo. Netta stopped in front of the white Ford Explorer in the parking lot. The sign on the side read ALS Realty: Antoinetta LaCrosse Skinner. The SUV was the first car she ever bought new and was proud of it. So proud, that she only drove it for business purposes. Netta had been in such a rush to see Bryce that she didn't notice it in the parking lot earlier.

Netta kept seeing that Ronnie's face. She wanted to wipe the smug expression right off of her face and she was looking at a way to do just that. Netta pulled her phone from her purse and dialed.

"Hello, I understand that you're looking for the driver of a white Ford Explorer that ran a Mrs. Lauren Malone off of the road. Well if you come to 8242 Ocean View Road, Apt. T, you will find the driver laid up under Bryce Wessler. Oh and you might want to send a car out for him too 'cause that fool's gettin' ready to skip town."

Chapter 46

Lauren heard voices coming from Eleanor's screened in porch so she headed towards the back of the house to find her aunt and Netta in a deep conversation.

"See, that's what you get for getting into bed with the enemy," Aunt Eleanor was saying as she wove the long sweet grass through the coil.

"It was all a setup, Granny," Netta told her. "You can't sell to him now."

"Just 'cause you got your face cracked doesn't mean I'm changing my mind about selling this place. It's too much money to turn down."

Lauren cleared her throat to make her presence known to her cousin and great aunt.

"Hello Lauren," Eleanor spoke not looking up from the basket she was weaving.

"Hello Aunt Eleanor. Hello Netta."

"Are you speaking to me?" Netta asked sarcastically. Clearly she had not forgotten her argument at church.

"Yeah, well you've made some very poor choices, but I'm not going to be rude and not speak when I see you."

"Fine whatever."

Awkwardness settled in between Lauren and Netta. Aunt Eleanor kept right on weaving. Lauren watched as she weaved. Aunt Eleanor had always been a skilled weaver. Her baskets of many shapes and sizes brought in a great price at the mainland market. Tourists really came out of the pocket for an authentic, hand-woven, sweet grass basket. They came in all shapes and sizes. Large, small, elongated, and flat. Some had handles, and some didn't. Some had lids and others were left open. Whatever the basket, each was an original masterpiece.

In the LaCrosse family, no one beyond Great Aunt Eleanor's generation learned the art of weaving baskets. When she left this earth, the skill would leave with her. Lauren was suddenly ashamed of herself for not taking the time to learn. Here she was accusing Netta of not keeping the land in the family and she herself couldn't maintain a tradition that had traveled from the Motherland of Africa and had been kept alive on the Sea Islands for many generations.

Aunt Eleanor's brusque voice suddenly interrupted Lauren's thoughts. "Are you two gonna stand around listenin' to each other breathe or y'all gonna say somethin'."

"Actually, I do have something to say," said Lauren.

"Oh great, more words from the self-righteous." Netta's tone was again sarcastic.

"I guess I deserved that," Lauren conceded. "I just wanted to say 'thank you.'"

"Oh yeah, for what? For proving once again that you are the smarter cousin who does everything right?" Netta asked bitterly. She was still raw from what happened with Bryce Wessler and his little prostitute, and she was no mood to let Lauren off the hook.

"Netta, will you give me a break?!" Lauren finally had enough of her tone. "I want to thank you for reporting the fool that ran me off the road!"

Netta looked away and grumbled, "You're welcome," as if pained her to say those two words.

"The cops told me that it was your assistant?" Lauren asked.

"Yeah, that little heffa used me for my connections with Wessler and the folks on Oak Grove Island. I guess that's what I get for sleeping with the enemy."

"Literarily," Aunt Eleanor interjected.

Netta glared at her grandmother, while Lauren tried not to look too shocked with that last bit of information. Eleanor continued her weaving, oblivious to the venomous stare Netta was aiming in her direction.

"Anyway, my assistant ran you off the road to win favor with Wessler."

"What do you mean, 'win favor'?" Lauren asked confused.

Netta sighed then told her cousin the humiliating details.

"I'm really sorry that happened to you," Lauren sympathized.

"You're sorry?" Netta was surprised. "I thought you would think that I was getting what I deserved."

"Well, no one deserves to get played. So…" Lauren tried to find a polite way to pose her next question. "What about Derek?"

"What about him?" Netta asked. "This had nothing to do with him and he doesn't need to know about it." She gave Lauren a pointed look.

"Hey. It's none of my business," said Lauren holding her hands up.

"That's right. It isn't."

"So how did you find out about your assistant anyway? It's not like a whole lot of people knew that it was a white SUV that ran me off the road."

Netta chuckled. "That fool assistant of mine took the car to Spunkie's auto body shop on the mainland to get it fixed. Spunkie is an old friend of Derek's. Remember Derek is a mechanic also. They used to work in the same garage back in the day. So when my assistant dropped off the company car, with the company initials on the side and the big dent in the front bumper, Spunkie was naturally concerned about his friend's wife and called to check up. I, of course, knew nothing about the dent and asked for details of how my car ended up at his shop. Spunkie told me that the woman who dropped it off said that *her boss* was in a hurry to go to a closing and accidentally ran off the road."

"Only you knew nothing about this accident," Lauren filled in. "And she didn't know that Derek is a mechanic and that you would have taken the car to his garage, not Spunkie's."

"Exactly. And she didn't know that Spunkie knew that I was ALS. So when I was completely surprised about the dent, he put it together that Randy wanted to keep the accident from her boss – me - and since he didn't owe her no favors he told me that the dent in the car didn't look like one that's sustained in running off the road but from striking another car several times. He also found paint on the fender."

"And from all of this you put together, that she was the one who tried to run me down?"

"I wasn't entirely sure although the time and the fact that she could have rear-ended someone fit," Netta continued. "This morning, I found Wessler and Randy together, when I showed up at the condo to finish up some business. So when Randy tried to humiliate me in front of Wessler, I called the police to get her back although I still wasn't entirely sure."

"Well she confessed to it."

"So I heard. You don't steal my accounts and benefit from the groundwork that I laid down and not expect for me to retaliate. Plus, I got that trick two times because I checked the real estate regs. She got the knowledge of Wessler's dealings while working for me as my assistant. Any money that she makes selling the new development, I get a cut."

Clearly that news was new to Eleanor. Although she continued to weave, Lauren detected a deep furrow in her brow.

Lauren chose her words to Netta very carefully. "Do you really want these people's blood money?"

"Lauren, I'm providing for my family. If I don't make this money, someone else will. I know you don't agree with me, but that's the way it is."

"No, I don't agree with you. But I do believe that you know that deep down all of that's happening with Oak Grove is wrong. I overheard you try to convince Aunt Eleanor not to sell her land."

"She can try and convince me until she's blue in the face but I made up my mind. I'm selling," Eleanor said, still weaving.

"Aunt Eleanor, even after what Netta told you about what Wessler did to her? He's a user! He used her and he'll use you too!"

"She doesn't care about that," Netta said scornfully. "She doesn't care that I hurt. Whatever. I'm out of here."

Netta stormed out.

That was good for Lauren because she really needed to speak to her aunt alone.

"Aunt Eleanor," Lauren spoke very purposely. "You really don't think that you can sell this property, do you?"

Aunt Eleanor, who had been working so intently the entire time Lauren and Netta were conversing, finally looked up from her weaving and stared at her great-niece.

"So you know too," she said and chuckled wryly.

"Know what?" Lauren wanted Aunt Eleanor to come right out and say it.

"That my sister-in-law owns my land. Seemed like every little body was let in on that secret."

"No, not everyone."

"Who do you think you are the island's savior?" Aunt Eleanor questioned. "Like Delmar thought he was?"

"I'm not trying to save the island, Aunt Eleanor. I have finally realized that I cannot do that anymore, but I can work hard to make sure the LaCrosse land stays in the in family like my Granddad Lazarus wanted."

"Lazarus!" Eleanor scoffed as she went back to her weaving. "Even from the grave that man is dictatin' how this family should be run. He didn't want my Micah to have nothin'!"

"Aunt Eleanor, you know that's not how this situation came about. Uncle Micah was in a bind."

"Ain't no bind big enough to sell our land without telling me!"

"I know that must be painful for you but you were never supposed to find out about the land being sold to my granddad. My grandparents didn't see the need for you to know. The land, as far as they were concerned, was still yours to live on. But you want to sell it, that's the only reason Grandma brought up the deed."

Eleanor laughed. "Henrietta didn't bring up the deed."

"She didn't?" Lauren was shocked. She definitely over-estimated Aunt Eleanor's intelligence in this situation.

"No."

"Then who did?"

"Delmar. He came here just like you did spouting out all this mess about Lazarus and the land and how I ain't s'posed to sell it on account of some promise he made."

"Yeah, we, Netta included, promised my Granddaddy Lazarus that we would not sell LaCrosse land ever."

"It ain't your decision! I'm tellin' you just like I told him!"

"And when you told Delmar of your decision to sell, that's when he told you about the deed?"

"Yeah. That boy told me that I couldn't sell *my* property because it belonged to Henrietta. He musta known I wouldn't believe him because he whips out a copy of the handwritten mess my weak-assed husband signed and the note that said he could buy it back when we got our mess together." Aunt Eleanor threw her unfinished basket to the side in frustration. "But we never could get anything together, not with them damn children suckin' us dry! One gets thrown in jail for this, the other in jail for that, they run up the debts, they lose money gamblin', even the baby Ellen needin' somethin'."

Yeah, she needed money for college tuition, Lauren thought to herself wondering how jail and college could be on the same level of need in Eleanor's mind.

"So what did you do when you saw Delmar with the handwritten deed?"

"Whatcha think I did! I told him to give it to me and not to speak of it again. But Delmar was always so damn stubborn. He refused to give it to me. He said he'd keep the deed a secret if I agreed just to live on the land and not sell it to developers. He was going to see to it that LaCrosse land stayed LaCrosse land. Who the hell did he think he was telling me what to do like he owned me?!"

"He wasn't telling you what to do, Aunt Eleanor," Lauren explained. "We were taught that land is the one thing black folks on this island could call theirs. No one could take it from us unless we gave it away. That's more valuable than money. You spend money and it's gone, but the land will live on forever. You have something for your children.

See, Uncle Micah understood that. He went to his brother with the land because he knew that it would stay in the family no matter how much trouble he was in. But you don't understand that there are more important things than money, so your kids don't understand it either. Even Netta who got into cahoots with Wessler still doesn't get the fact that she traded in her pride, self-respect, and possibly her marriage for a few dollars. But maybe you backed her into that corner, Auntie, seeing that you refused to give her anything."

"See that's what I'm talking about right there!" Aunt Eleanor pointed an accusatory finger at Lauren.

"What Aunt Eleanor? Just what are you talking about?" Lauren came back at her.

"Delmar talked to me in that same self-righteous tone. When I went to his office that night, I told him that I wanted the deed and he thought he could put me in my place!"

"What night?" Lauren asked trying to keep control, though at this point she was feeling anything but. "The night Delmar was *killed*?"

Eleanor realized she'd said too much. "T-That was an accident, okay."

"He's dead. How's that an accident?"

"I pulled out the gun to scare him into giving me the deed."

"Let me get this straight. You pulled a gun on your own nephew?" Lauren blinked several times trying to process this information.

"Just to scare 'im!" Aunt Eleanor tried to explain desperately. "Them developers was gonna pay me a lot of money for this property. They promised to name the place LaCrosse Plantation and I would get a condo to rent for two months out of the year for the rest of my life. That's a great deal."

Lauren said nothing and Eleanor continued to explain her actions. "I been waitin' to get off this island since the day before forever. Since I was a girl, I fished and farmed and weaved my life away on this island. Then I married Micah and I was still fishin' and farmin' and weavin'. I didn't get to do nothin' else. Everything we owned, my kids took. Then they left me with the grandkids and I continued to have nothin'. With this offer Wessler made me, I was going to finally get a chance to get away from all of that. I was gonna retire in Florida and not have to worry about nothin' for the rest of my life. Then Delmar had to go and ruin it for me! I just wanted the deed!"

Finally Lauren spoke. "Are you the one that trashed his office?"

"I needed to find that deed."

"Was this before or after you shot your great nephew in cold blood."

Lauren could barely hear Eleanor when she said, "After."

"Why did you take his rezoning files? What did that have to do with what you were after, or was that just a way to point the finger at someone else?"

"I don't know nothin' about any files! Somebody else musta come after I left!"

"What about his apartment?"

"It was a total mess when I got there. I just ripped the furniture and took down the books in case he hid the deed in the house. I was lookin' in the bedroom when you showed up. Messed up my knee gettin' through that window."

"That was *you*?"

"Yeah and when I heard the door close, I thought you left but you didn't."

Lauren sighed angrily. She could not believe that it was her great-aunt that had chased her out of Delmar's apartment.

"Where did you get the gun, Aunt Eleanor?" Lauren asked coldly.

"It was Torrin's. I got it out of his room."

"Uh-huh and where is it now?" Lauren wanted to make sure they weren't anywhere near it before they had another "accident".

"I buried it out in the watermelon patch."

"So you just left him there?" Lauren cried.

"What?" Eleanor was confused.

"Delmar! Did you just leave Delmar bleeding in the middle of his office floor and didn't even try to help him?"

"He was going to tell about the deed!"

"So was my grandma. Were you going to kill her too?"

"I didn't know that she knew," Eleanor said quietly. "I figured if Micah didn't tell me about the deed, then Lazarus didn't tell Henrietta. You know how men are about their business. I figured with Delmar dead, my secret was safe and I would sell the land like I planned."

"She knew," said Lauren, her voice still cold. "Where do you think Delmar got the deed from in the first place?"

"Figured he found it in Lazarus's old papers or somethin'."

"It's in a very safe place." Lauren stood up. "And just so you don't get any ideas about killing off anymore family members, I will inform you that the deed is in a safe deposit box far away from here. Also, I plan to convince the family to hire a lawyer to have the property properly recorded in Henrietta's name. Don't worry, though. Your family will be allowed to remain. And as for your 'accident,' it looks to me that Florida is out of the question. You'll most likely live out the rest of your days with the State of South Carolina."

"You're gonna tell on me?!" Aunt Eleanor asked incredulously. "I'm eighty-five years old and you're gonna send me to jail?"

"Are you even serious to ask me that question? Aunt Eleanor, you killed your great-nephew!"

"I told you it was an accident!"

"That accident left my best friend and cousin dead. Someone's got to answer for that. If not you, then who?"

With that, Lauren turned and walked out of the screened in porch. Although she didn't remember how she got there, somehow she made it across the freshly cut green yard.

"Did you get all of that?" Lauren asked.

The police chief of Oak Grove Island stepped out of a grove of low-growing palmetto trees where he was hiding and pulled off his headset.

He nodded and said, "I got every word." Then he picked up his walkie-talkie and said, "Go and get her boys."

Chapter 47

Kyle ran over to his wife and held her tightly.

"I was holding my breath the entire time you were in there!" he exclaimed.

"I was scared too," said Lauren, her voice muffled by Kyle's chest.

"You didn't sound like it. You were practically a pro." He finally let go of his wife.

"That part was easy. Aunt Eleanor was always easy to get a rise out of, especially if you come across like you know more than she does. She especially hates that. Then once I got her that angry, I just led her where I wanted her to go."

Lauren's words trailed off as they caught sight of a couple of officers leading Aunt Eleanor out of the house with her hands cuffed behind her.

"You old bat!" Netta screeched as she too stepped out of the grove of trees.

When Netta had walked off the porch after the confrontation with her grandmother, she intended to head towards her car and go home. However, she'd turned back towards the porch to try again to convince her grandmother not to sell her property. The police, fearing that Netta would compromise the operation, intercepted her and hurried her into the hiding place, where she caught the gist of the conversation between her grandmother and Lauren. Netta was beside herself when the police confirmed what they'd heard in their headsets: That Eleanor had gunned down Delmar.

"Netta, this don't even concern you, so go back to your husband while you still have one."

Netta gave her grandmother an incredulous look. "Don't concern me?! Delmar was my cousin! I loved him!"

"He didn't love you. You were just the odd-ball cousin he put up with," Eleanor said coldly.

Netta met her cold glance with one of her own. "Why do you hate me so much?"

Eleanor looked as if she were surprised by the question, but she recovered quickly. Lauren will never forget as long as she lived the answer her great-aunt gave to Netta's question.

"Your sisters understood a long time ago that I didn't want them living with me and they minded their own business. They stayed out of my way and got out of my house the moment they turned eighteen. You? You always acted like I was supposed to be your mama. You was always expectin' somethin' out of me. You never got that after raisin' my own kids, I had nothin' left to give you!"

Netta for only an instant looked like she'd been stabbed in the heart, but only for an instant.

Netta's voice was very clear when she responded, "Well, you certainly can't give me a damn thing behind bars. Have a nice life...*Granny*."

With those last words, the officers opened up the back door to the squad car and gently guided her in. The slam of the car door echoed across the yard. Kyle, Lauren, and Netta, who standing a short distance from them, watched silently as the police cars drove away with red lights flashing.

Chapter 48

It had been three days since Jefferson's operation. Lauren and Kyle had gone by the hospital to find that he was still in the intensive care unit. They couldn't officially visit. Only family was allowed in ICU, but an old school nurse friend of Lauren's snuck the two of them in and the couple stared at Jefferson through the observation window.

"He still looks so sick," said Lauren quietly.

"No one looks well with tubes and I.V.s running out of their body, Babe," said Kyle putting his arms around her. "I'm sure it's not as bad as it looks."

"His mother said that the doctors are hoping he wakes up in the next day or two but the longer he's unconscious, the more likely he is to stay that way. Then they said something about exploring other options. I wasn't sure I wanted to know what that meant, and I had a feeling that Mrs. Pierce didn't want to go there with me either."

"We just need to keep praying, Lauren. Jefferson's strong. He'll come out of this okay."

"Did I tell you that Bryce Wessler is back in jail?"

"What?" Kyle exclaimed. "What happened?"

"The police caught that fool trying to jump bail the same time they arrested Netta's assistant for trying to run me over. Serves him right for the way he messed over Netta."

"Wow," said Kyle in disbelief. "Yeah, you told me about the assistant but what is this about Netta hooking up with Wessler also?"

"It was like one big triangle," Lauren said, shaking her head. "Netta's still feeling pretty humiliated."

"But she's going to hold on to that money, huh?"

"That's what she's saying."

"Maybe she feels she doesn't have a choice, Lauren," said Kyle. "And now that Aunt Eleanor lost her property, Netta really feels like she needs something that's hers."

Lauren sighed. "I see what you're saying."

"So you think Wessler's going to do time for shooting Jefferson?"

"Honestly?"

"Yes, be honest."

"No, I do not."

Chapter 49

John, Marne, Lauren, Kyle and Justin let themselves in through the screened porch of Henrietta's House. They could hear the festivities inside even before they opened the door. Because of the impromptu family dinner, Lauren and Kyle decided to stay one more day on Oak Grove Island.

In his grandpapa's arms dressed in his best little short set and sandals was Justin. His Godparents were thoughtful enough to bring him down to the island. They'd declined the invitation to dinner at the LaCrosse's. Instead they got a hotel room with a river view on the mainland.

"Here they are!" exclaimed Aunt Jessie hugging all of them.

"And they brought the baby!" piped up Aunt Philomena, stooping down to his level. "Come and give your Auntie a kiss."

John set his grandson down and Justin hid behind his mother's leg.

"Justin say, hello to Aunt Philomena." Lauren prompted Justin retreated further behind her. "Go on."

"Hi," Justin said timidly, as he peeked out from around Lauren.

"Hi sweetheart," Aunt Philomena cooed.

The other aunts, uncles, and cousins followed suit. They all missed Justin and it wasn't very often they got to see him.

"If we could gather around the table and bless the food," Uncle Izzie spoke over the noise. The family crowded around. The long table looked amazing with all kinds of good things to eat. There was chicken, salads, pork chops, white rice, red rice, okra, green beans, and macaroni and cheese. Lauren counted at least five different desserts on the table and planned to sample all of them (if she could beat Aunt Philomena and Aunt Tessie to the table.)

"Before we bless the food, I would like to say a few things," said Grandma Henrietta spoke. "This has been a hard few weeks for the family."

Everyone looked over at Delmar's parents. "Yes it has," cried Aunt Dinah.

"And there is some sense of closure because we found out the truth about what happened to Delmar. I'm sad to say that the truth of who killed him has been almost as painful as his passing."

Several family members nodded.

"While we may feel some ill will towards Eleanor for what she did, we must be sure the it doesn't extend to the rest of her family, because in spite of everything, they're still family. They still share our blood."

"Unfortunately," Tiny grumbled. Several members of the family shared her negative sentiment.

"Don't be that way, Tiny," John spoke up. "Mom's right. We can't punish all of Micah and Eleanor's children.

"I agree," said Uncle Thomas, Delmar's father. "Being evil towards them won't bring back my son. I personally can't hold onto that hate. What keeps me going is my pride in Delmar. He died protecting our family from a horrible fate. His cousin Lauren, with the help of her husband, refused to let the truth he discovered be buried with him and I am grateful. So I don't want to spend the evening talking about Eleanor. The Lord's gonna take care of her in the way He sees fit. Right now, I just want to raise my glass to family.

The family raised their glasses also. "To family…"

Just then there was a knock at the door. Tessie opened the door. It was Netta. The family was so silent, the sound of the waves in the distance, was the only sound in the room. Then Netta spoke.

"I-I didn't mean to intrude. I just came by to say that I-I am so sorry for what my grandmother's done. I am speaking for the rest of my family when I say this. I don't blame you if you never want to see me again…" Her voice trailed off.

"Come right on in, Netta," said Henrietta extending her hand to her great-niece and guided her into the room. "You don't have to apologize for anything."

"Doesn't she?" asked Tiny. "She made a whole lot of people sell off their land."

"No she didn't." Lauren spoke up, catching her cousin's eye. "Netta can't make anyone do anything they don't want to do."

Lauren glanced over at her father who gave a slight approving nod. "People have to decide on their own whether or not to sell. We can't do anything about them, but we can do something about us. We can decide not to sell and hope that other grandchildren have had talks with their grandfathers about what their land means to them. Maybe if we're lucky, they made and kept promises like the one Delmar, Netta, and I made to Granddad Lazarus, not to sell the land. If we have enough people like that on this island, then maybe we have a fighting chance against developers. But it's up to the individual."

"Amen," said Grandma Henrietta clapping her hands together.

"For right now, there's a lot of good food that's getting cold and I, for one, am ready to eat. Grab a plate, Netta. This is a family dinner."

Aunt Tiny handed Netta a plate.

After the blessing, Netta spoke one word in Lauren's ear. "Thanks."

One year later…

"Justin, it's time to come on in and say hello to your great-grandmother."

"Couple more minutes, Mama," Justin said as he reached for a thick sprawling branch.

Lauren sat down on a lower branch and watched her son. "You really love this old tree don't you?"

Justin's answer came in loud giggles as he flipped his long three-year-old body upside down. Lauren and Kyle laughed with him. It had been a good year. Lauren finally found a job with a planning firm in Macon. Kyle's business continued to flourish. The LaCrosse family was successful at keeping the Wessler-Forest Corporation at bay and all 1,000 acres remained intact. Unfortunately, Netta had bought a total of 3,000 acres for Bryce Wessler. Now new exclusive luxury development began popping up all over Oak Grove Island. Areas where islanders had once roamed free were no longer accessible as manned gates blocked the entrances.

It also looked as if Telly Whitman would be able to get all of the votes he needed by the time the mayoral election rolled around in another year. The only hope the islanders had was if the charges of him intimidating the council members actually stuck. The trial was to begin in a couple of months. It was looking bleak, however. It seemed everyday a witness would recant his or her statement against Whitman.

On the upside, Dee and Carlos Rashad were released when Eleanor was arrested for Delmar's murder. They settled on the old Walter Simpson property that belonged to them and built a new house. The conservation subdivision planned for that end of the island was on hold until the new plans could be drafted that respected the property lines and avoided the cemetery. Wessler's investors were less than pleased with the delay. Lauren was continuing the work that Delmar had begun and was still researching the possibility of declaring the old graveyard on the site as a historical landmark.

As for Bryce Wessler, he actually saw the inside of a courthouse and went on trial for Jefferson's shooting. As Lauren had predicted, Wessler was acquitted and free to make trouble in some other desirable location. The day after the conclusion of the trial, Wessler's condo exploded. He'd escaped injury for he disappeared the moment the charges were dismissed. The rumors were that he was buying acres on a remote island in Georgia. That didn't sit too well with Lauren, but she believed that Wessler would not be able to get away with his dirty dealings for too much longer.

Jefferson woke up two days after Lauren and Kyle left for Macon. Physical therapy had been painful and slow, but he made a full recovery. He was back on the police force and he'd earned the respect of his fellow officers, particularly Clyde, who had stopped giving him a hard time about his detective status.

Lauren and Netta were friends again for the time being. With Delmar no longer there to patch up their arguments, the cousins had finally learned to work things out for themselves. Lauren realized that she and Netta had different philosophies of life. She would have to accept that about Netta and decide that their relationship was more important than holding on so tightly to what Lauren thought was wrong and right.

It came as no surprise to anyone that Eleanor LaCrosse was sentenced to 25 years to life in prison by a jury of her peers. As Lauren had promised Eleanor, Henrietta LaCrosse sought to have the unrecorded deed made by Lazarus and Micah, official. All 1,000 acres now belonged to Henrietta LaCrosse and would be passed down to her family. The promise made to Lazarus had been honored after all. He and Delmar could rest easy.

"You know, Justin, your mama used to play here with Delmar when she was a girl," Kyle told his son who was still flipping over thick branches.

Justin stopped flipping. "Who's Delmar?" He asked.

Lauren spied the red stain on the branch and realized there was so much to tell her son about her favorite cousin, but for now she said, "He was my blood cousin."

"Do I have a blood cousin?"

Lauren pulled Justin out of the tree and held his long, agile body in her arms and answered, "Only if you're really lucky."

Acknowledgements

I would like to thank my husband, Kevin who knew of my dream to become a writer almost from the moment we met. He has always been there to support me and he is a wonderful person to bounce book ideas off of. I want to send love to my parents, Joseph and Julie Grant who have always nurtured my love of writing and taught me the importance of leaving a legacy. I especially would like to thank my sister, Tarisse Grant-Shelton for her wonderful artwork on the cover. She could end up being the newest featured Low Country artist. My UNO Girls, determined that I would get published gave me information to every literary contact imaginable. Lastly, I would like to dedicate this book posthumously to my wonderful grandmother Janie Aiken Grant, a storyteller in her own right, who gave me the inspiration to tell this story.